The
TEQUILA
WORM
Viola Canales

WENDY
LAMB
BOOKS

Published by
Wendy Lamb Books
an imprint of
Random House Children's Books
a division of Random House, Inc.
New York

Visit us on the Web! www.randomhouse.com/teens
Educators and librarians, for a variety of teaching tools, visit us at
www.randomhouse.com/teachers

Library of Congress Cataloging-in-Publication Data is available upon request.

ISBN: 0-385-74674-1 (trade)
0-385-90905-5 (lib. bdg.)

The text of this book is set in 12.5-point Adobe Caslon.

Book design by Angela Carlino

Printed in the United States of America

August 2005

10 9 8 7 6 5 4 3 2 1

BVG

To Antonio Canales, my late father,
for teaching me to follow my dreams.

To Dora Casas Canales, my mother,
for teaching me to love.

To Pamela Karlan, my best friend,
for being Pam.

To Wendy Lamb, my editor,
for making this book possible.

And to all comadres and compadres . . .

Acknowledgments

I thank my lovely agent, Andrea Brown.

I also thank the wonderful teachers, staff, and students of Saint Stephen's Episcopal School, and most of all Dr. Flory, who made it possible for me to attend this terrific, caring school.

Last, I thank all my family and friends, especially those who helped inspire this story: Veronica Canales, Antonio Canales Jr., Gustavo Canales, Gloria Tijerina, Sandra Canales, Minta Rivas, Consuelo Canales, Hilda Canales, Cecilia Canales, Gonzaga Vela, Lile Casas, Miguel Casas, Lucy Casas, Sara Bowser, Dinah Acord, and Irma Muñoz.

The STORYTELLER'S BAG

In the evenings when the cool breeze began to blow, all the families came out to their porches to sit and talk, to laugh and gossip. And that is where and how our barrio became one family.

Doña Clara visited every summer and *no one* missed *her* stories, for she came carrying a bag filled with secret things that conjured up the most amazing tales.

Clara had a square face on top of a big round body, and the biggest eyes and the widest mouth: she was especially proud of her catfish mouth, which she painted scarlet. She wore a big black onyx tongue around her neck.

"This," she said, "is the symbol of a storyteller. It has been handed down from generation to generation, for hundreds of years."

When asked where she'd come from, she'd roll her eyes, pitch her arms up to the night sky, and point to the stars with her long scarlet fingernails. So the other kids and I believed she'd just flown down from a star.

Then she'd shake her many wooden bracelets and thrust her hand into her mysterious bag. She rattled her things around as we stared, bug-eyed.

Clara sucked her front teeth, batted her eyes, and then slowly started lifting something out of her bag. You could hear your blood go *thump! thump! thump!*

Once, she pulled out a three-inch lock of hair. "This belonged to Mama Maria, your great-great-grandmother."

As the lock of dark hair made its way from hand to hand, person to person, Clara said, "Your Mama Maria was a mule. Always kicking her way through things. A force to behold! But beautiful, with the darkest eyes and long, wild Apache hair. *This hair.*

"And you, Sofia"—Clara pointed at me—"not only look like her, but have inherited her gift for mule-kicking." I gasped. My cousin Berta laughed.

Papa was sitting beside me on top of an upside-down pail. "*Mi'ja,* don't look so worried. This is a good thing— for things to kick will come your way in many shapes and sizes. You'll see."

Next Clara pulled out a jar full of big mule teeth with a piece of a blue balloon inside. "I always show the hair and teeth and blue balloon together," she said, "for the teeth belonged to Papa Carlos, your great-great-grandfather, Mama Maria's husband, and he gave this blue balloon to her when they met and fell in love in a little Mexican plaza far away. The town plaza, in those days, was where people gathered to tell their tales."

Oh no! I thought. *Please don't say I inherited those teeth, too!*

But Clara pointed at Berta, who bit her lip and covered her big mouth with her hand. Now *I* laughed.

"*Hija,* the big teeth are a good gift too," said Berta's mother, Tía Belia, "if you learn to use them right."

And as the jar of teeth made its way around, Clara told us, "Look closely at them, for they once bit a rattlesnake in half, chewed a mountain of tobacco, and helped yell out the longest string of insults imaginable.

"Yes, kicking and biting like mules runs deep in our blood. Never forget that, for it might come in handy someday."

The things Clara pulled out of her bag included chipped saints, wacky handmade dolls, arrowheads, recipes, cracked old photos of stiff people, and pictures of dead children, who looked beautiful and peacefully asleep.

Clara always stayed a couple of days and then disappeared. "I have to go visit other families, other barrios, for it's important that they also hear these stories."

But before leaving she'd reach into her bag one last time to pull out a tiny bottle of mescal. She'd take a hairpin and fish out the tequila worm swimming inside. "This will cure my homesickness as I travel to my next family," Clara would say, popping the tequila worm into her mouth and chewing. She swallowed loudly as we stared. I was amazed. Sick, too. "Now, is there some story you want me to tell as I continue on my journey?"

I'd shake my head. There was nothing I'd want her to tell, at least nothing that could possibly compare with the stories that went with the big teeth, the lock of hair, and especially the tequila worm.

When I was about six, Clara came to visit as usual, but this time she was in a wheelchair. And when we gathered around her on the porch, we saw that her big mouth had collapsed into a thin line and her popping eyes gazed out at nothing.

Mama kissed Clara's trembling white hair and placed her story bag at the center of the porch. She reached inside and slowly pulled out her cupped hand. There was nothing in it. But Mama handed the invisible thing to me and said, "Here is the ceramic baby Jesus for the manger of the Christmas *nacimiento* your *abuelita* builds each year. It represents the vivid image Clara gave me of my great-grandmother Maria, who I never met, but who I feel close to through her story: about how she worked for weeks, making tamales and then going door to door selling them so she could buy a brand-new baby Jesus for her daughter, my mother, who was appointed the Christmas *madrina*, the godmother for baby Jesus that year." This image was passed around from hand to hand, person to person.

"Sofia, you're next!" Mama said. "Reach into the bag and see what secret is inside for you." I put my hand in and felt all around. *Empty.* I pulled out my cupped hand and showed everyone. I hesitated, then turned to look at Clara. "This is the black onyx tongue that Clara still wears around her neck. I look at it and remember all the stories Clara has told us. Our stories."

"Yes," said Mama. "Clara is a perfect example of a good *comadre.*"

"A good *comadre*?" I said.

"Someone who makes people into a family. And it's what I want you and your little sister, Lucy, to grow up to be."

"But, *mi'ja*, don't worry about this *now*," Papa said, smiling and tapping out a waltz on the cement floor with his brand-new brown and white cowboy boots. "It's something you'll gradually pick up along the way."

Mama handed Clara's bag to my cousin Berta. "It's your turn."

That night, as I lay awake, I thought about Clara and what Mama had said about becoming a good *comadre*. All I could figure out was that telling stories was a big part of the secret to becoming one. That, and being brave enough to eat a whole tequila worm.

The Candy Bite

One Saturday morning, I walked into the kitchen and told Mama, "I'm not going to be friends with Berta anymore. She's mean and selfish." I still hadn't figured out what being a good *comadre* was all about, but I was sure I didn't want to make Berta part of *my* family.

"But Berta's your cousin, your best friend," Mama said as she stopped sweeping and turned to look at me. "You've played together since you were babies."

"She might still be my cousin, but she's not my best friend anymore." I went into the living room and started watching cartoons.

There was a knock on the front door. I glanced out the window and saw Berta's hazel eyes and the red bow in her curly brown hair. I raced into the kitchen.

"It's Berta. Tell her I'm not here."

"You go tell her. What? I'm supposed to lie for you now?"

"Oh, *please*. I'll sweep the rest of the kitchen for you."

"I'll consider it if you tell me why all of a sudden you've stopped liking Berta."

Berta knocked louder. "Sofia! Sofia! Are you home?"

"Berta always takes a huge bite out of my candy bars, but when she has one she puts her fingers on the tip so I can only take the tiniest nibble out of hers."

Mama shook her head. "*Mi'ja* . . . go get two nickels from my purse and then take Berta to the store to buy *two* candy bars—one for you and one for her."

The very next day Mama and I were walking to church for seven o'clock Sunday Mass. I turned and saw Berta on the other side of the street, about ten paces ahead of us. She was eating a chocolate bar. I glared at her, my mouth watering. Then I got mad.

"Is that Berta?" Mama looked at me.

"Yeah."

"Eating a candy bar—right?"

Silence.

"Sofia, why don't you go over and ask her to give you a bite?"

I started walking more slowly, letting Mama go ahead.

"Sofia, I'm talking to you."

"What?"

"Go over and ask Berta for a bite of her chocolate."

"I . . . don't want . . . any."

"Oh, Sofia, don't try that on me. I know you like your papa knows his bean pot. You're *loca* about candy—chocolate especially. Now go over and get a bite. Remember, you bought her a whole candy bar yesterday."

"But she'll only let me take a nibble."

"Well, if she puts her fingers at the tip again, you have my permission to go ahead and bite them."

What?

"I'm serious. Now go on." Mama turned me toward Berta and gave me a push.

I turned to Mama. She waved me off. I slowly crossed the street and turned to Mama again. Still serious.

Berta was absorbed in her chocolate bar. I felt my blood hot and rushing, my hands sweaty.

"Hey, Berta . . ."

She turned, her nostrils flared. She made her eyes into slits. "Oh . . . hi."

I turned to Mama. She had caught up to us but was still across the street. Still serious.

"Berta . . . can I . . . have a bite?"

Berta sighed like a big balloon letting out air. "Okay . . ." She took her candy bar and put her fingers on the tip.

Mama nodded.

I took a huge bite. Berta howled and took a bite of my shoulder.

I kicked her like a mule. I didn't even bother to turn to look at Mama then.

As Berta's big teeth came at me for another bite, her mother, Tía Belia, miraculously appeared and pulled her back. Mama caught me as I was about to kick Berta on her butt.

We stood in our mothers' arms, panting, glaring, with sweaty red faces. Berta clutched her candy bar like a trophy.

"Berta," said her mother, "now, share your chocolate with Sofia. Remember that she bought you a whole candy bar yesterday. Break it in half and give her a piece."

Berta squinted.

"*Berta . . .*"

With tears in her eyes, she took off the wrapper and snapped the candy bar in two. One piece was much bigger than the other.

"Give your friend Sofia a piece." Berta handed me the smaller piece. "Wait. Sofia, you take the piece you want."

I gulped, looked at Berta's watery eyes, and took the smaller piece.

THE HOLY HOST

BEFORE making my First Communion at seven, I practiced taking the holy host using a roll of Necco candy wafers. The roll was wrapped in clear crinkly paper and the wafers, as big and thin as quarters, lay one next to the other, like coins in a roll, purple and pink, orange, yellow, green, and white.

When we played "taking the holy host," I was the priest. My little sister, Lucy, and Berta's little brother, Noe, both three years old, were the penitents. I never asked Berta to play because she always ate most of the wafers, even if it was *my* roll of Neccos.

"This is serious business," I'd tell Lucy and Noe, "for you're practicing to take Jesus's body and blood. So pay attention!"

Lucy's bright brown eyes and Noe's dark ones squinted.

But I always knew they were just playing along to eat the candy wafers. When they burped or laughed, I said, "Stop fooling around! Just pure and holy behavior, or you might make the whole world come to a big crashing end!

"At catechism they teach you," I continued, "that the world will come to an end when a nun—and I mean *any* nun—dies. And the nuns who come pick you up at school to walk you over to catechism each and every Tuesday are all rickety old. So it won't take much to rattle them. And if you make an old, rattled nun angry, she might just croak right there and then."

Lucy and Noe would immediately stop giggling or pushing each other. I always took this opportunity to remind them, "Stop thinking that nuns are sweet and kind like Maria in *The Sound of Music*. That's just a movie. Think of the evil old *bruja* in 'Hansel and Gretel.'

"To take the holy host, you first have to make your First Holy Communion," I told them. "You also have to go and confess your sins—and I mean *all* your sins—to the priest, who hides behind a secret screen, inside a closet that looks like a big coffin—with you on the other side of the screen. Then you have to do your penance, which is whatever punishment the priest gives you for all your sins.

And if they're really, really bad, you might have to say hundreds, even thousands of Our Fathers and Hail Marys."

Their eyes widened.

"Then on Sunday," I continued, "you can't eat anything—not even a tiny crumb—for a whole hour before taking communion. When the Mass finally comes to the Communion part, which is soon after the priest raises a white wafer the size of a big tortilla to the heavens, you get in line, pew by pew, and then start making your way up the aisle in the Communion line, while you clasp your hands in prayer, bow your head, and try to look holy and such.

"And when you finally get to the very front of the altar and find yourself smack in front of the priest, who is holding this big gold goblet full of holy hosts, you close your eyes and stick out your tongue. The priest says something, you say something, and then the priest puts the host on the tip of your tongue. Then you quickly slip your tongue back into your mouth and head back to your pew, where you kneel and hold your hands in prayer and look holy.

"Now listen, it's very, very important that you let the host dissolve slowly in your mouth. You can't start chewing it like it's a piece of pork or something. Remember, it's Jesus's body and blood. And never, *never* can you stick out your tongue to show the host to anybody, much less touch it."

"But why not?" Lucy asked, her little round face serious.

"Because it's holy," I said.

"But what happens if you accidentally bite it or you

trip and it just pops out of your mouth?" Noe asked, scratching his head.

"You die and go to hell."

"Right then and there, or when you get old?"

"Right then and there. The ground opens up and swallows you whole."

"But why?" Lucy asked.

"Because it's *holy*. And that's what I've learned at catechism," I said, more and more annoyed.

I took all the white wafers from the Necco roll, put them inside a big yellow cup, and practiced giving Lucy and Noe the host until all the white wafers were gone. I then ate all the others.

Weeks after making my First Holy Communion, I was standing in the Communion line, my head bowed, my hands folded in prayer, when I panicked. I remembered taking a bite, a big bite, of Berta's chocolate bar just before Mass. Without her fat fingers this time. I'd thought nothing about it then, except for Berta's odd smirk. I secretly glanced at my Timex watch—a Communion gift from my parents. It was less than an hour since I'd taken the bite!

Oh no! What do I do? I couldn't take Communion now. I should just get out of line and go sit down. But what would people think? It would be a sign that I'd done something really, really evil.

I started sweating. My clasped hands trembled as I moved farther and farther up the Communion line toward the priest holding his big gold goblet. Since he was God's representative, he'd just know a whole hour hadn't passed when he got to me.

Then it kicked in: this might even be the death of me! It could be that the earth would open up the very second the priest put the host on my tongue. My breathing got faster and faster.

When I looked up, I found myself smack in front of the priest. I stood frozen, looking at my warped reflection on the shiny gold cup.

"The body of Christ," the priest said.

But nothing came out of me. "The body of Christ," he repeated, which was my signal to say "Amen," to open my mouth, and to stick out my tongue.

I just stood there, stunned. I desperately wanted to open my mouth, not to say "Amen" but to tell the priest, "I can't say 'Amen' because I don't want to die!"

I felt the host being shoved into my mouth and felt myself being pushed to the side. With the host still hanging partly out of my mouth, I quickly brought my hand up and secretly slipped the wafer into my shirt pocket.

I hurried back to my pew, went through the kneeling and praying. But there was no way to fake looking holy. As I knelt, I looked out of the corners of my eyes to see if anyone knew I was carrying Jesus's body and blood in my pocket.

When I finally got home, I said, "I'm not feeling well, I'm going to lie down." I changed into a T-shirt and carefully hung up my shirt, making sure the holy host was still safe inside the little pocket.

I said no to lunch and later to dinner, even after Mama fussed and prepared my favorite dish—a big batch of cheese enchiladas. She came and sat down on my bed. Her light brown hair smelled like a flower and she wore a bright yellow dress. She looked at me with her big brown eyes, like Lucy's. She felt my forehead. "No fever. But you look gray. And you always look gray when you're hiding something, Sofia." I shook my head until I couldn't keep it in anymore. I burst out crying. "I don't want to die! I don't want to get swallowed up by the ground!"

I finally told her—in fits and starts and hiccups—what had happened. Mama went to my closet and got my shirt.

"Mama, don't look in the pocket! You could die, too!" She took the shirt, still on the hanger, to the next room.

When she came back she said, "I called the priest, and he wants us to come over right away."

I turned blue with fright, but Mama said, "Don't worry, Sofia, the ground is not going to swallow you up."

At the rectory, I waited in the foyer while Mama went in to see the priest, carrying the shirt.

I had never felt so frightened in my life.

After a long, long time, Mama appeared, without my shirt. "We need to walk over to the church to pray." Once there, she said, "I must pray the fourteen Stations of the Cross." This is what Mama had to do—her punishment—so that I wouldn't get swallowed up. And as I followed her from station to station in the cold church full of shadows, I said my own secret prayers, for only grown-ups knew how to pray the Stations of the Cross. I also kept thanking God for giving me such a mama.

Later that night Berta came over for a cup of Mexican chocolate. *Still smirking.* But then she heard my story.

"Sorry, Sofia," Berta said, showing her big teeth. "I *never* thought you'd *die* when I offered you a bite."

I glared. Mama gave me a look, so I didn't kick Berta.

Three months later a strange box arrived in the mail, with no return address. Mama opened it and pulled out my shirt. And when I looked at the little pocket, I saw that it had been sewn shut.

EASTER CASCARONES

IT was Lent. I stayed close to Mama as she stood in front of her big cast-iron skillet, a carton of eggs next to the stove. She took an egg, turned its pointy end to the top, and then went *tap! tap! tap!* all around with a teaspoon. She peeled off the pieces of eggshell, leaving a small hole, and poured the egg into the frying pan, which was sizzling with oil and slices of onion. The egg white fell into the pan like a waterfall in slow motion, and the bright orange ball finally popped out.

Mama handed me the empty eggshell. While she did the same thing to the second egg, I carefully washed out the shell. I set it on the windowsill by the kitchen sink, its little hole facing down so it could dry.

We did this to the other seven eggs Mama used to make breakfast that morning.

We ate eggs, eggs, and nothing but eggs all during Lent. And although my favorite eggs were sunny side up, eggs with a happy face, during those weeks I ate only scrambled or sometimes very soft-boiled eggs.

I didn't mind, because this meant that many more cartons of *cascarones* for Easter.

As the forty days of Lent marched on, towers of egg cartons grew on top of the refrigerator. Seven days before Easter, I counted fifteen cartons.

"We've won! We've won!" I yelled, jumping up and down.

But then Berta walked in. *"Fifteen?* That's *nothing.* We've got seventeen," she said, baring her big fat teeth.

"Liar!" No one could possibly be eating more eggs than we were.

I rushed across the street to her house and counted and then recounted the cartons on top of her refrigerator. *Seventeen!*

"Cheater!" I said. "Some of those cartons are empty! Or missing some."

I ran home. "We aren't eating enough eggs!" I told Papa, who was sitting in the kitchen, tuning his old guitar.

Papa laughed and shook his dark-haired head. "*Mi'ja,* we have *too many* eggs already. You'll see, especially when it's time for you and your little sister to turn them into *cascarones* on Good Friday."

That evening I secretly poured a whole carton of eggs down the kitchen sink.

On Good Friday, Papa called me and Lucy to the porch. "Mama did her part, collecting all these eggs. Now it's *your* turn."

He moved the rocking chair and the plants in coffee cans to one side. Then he handed us a stack of old newspapers and helped us spread them on the cement floor. Lucy and I brought out the egg cartons—twenty! Papa appeared with a big brown paper bag.

As Lucy and I sat on the porch, the stacks of egg cartons towering around us, Papa sat down on an overturned pail. He opened a carton and handed an eggshell to each of us.

He put his eggshell onto his left index finger like a finger puppet. He opened the bag, took out a red crayon, and quickly drew a bird on the egg. With a pink crayon, he drew a flower, and gave it a green stem and two leaves. The yellow crayon produced a butterfly.

Papa spun his pretty egg around on his finger. We clapped as he placed it back inside the carton, its small hole pointing up. He popped another egg on his finger.

He took the black crayon and drew piercing eyes like

the Mexican revolutionary hero Zapata, bushy eyebrows, long nose, smiling mouth. Then a pencil-thin mustache. He colored dark brown hair on the sides and back.

"Your *Papa!*" he said, laughing, as he spun the egg and then put it into the carton.

A third egg was colored orange. His fourth was decorated with bright blue stars. The fifth became a pinto bean, spots and all. Then Papa stood up. "Your turn. Start coloring, use your imaginations. I'll stop by to check on you."

My first egg broke completely as I tried to draw a purple cat. The second egg was actually going quite well until I tried coloring near the top and the little hole became a huge gaping one. Then I just put a bunch of polka dots and checkmarks all over my eggs. I also drew a face or two, although I could never get the eyes to look like eyes, especially on the egg I did of Berta. But I got her big fat teeth right.

And Lucy was doing *even worse!* If only I had an older sister, one who could be *helpful.*

Lucy drew our cousin Linda dancing at her recent *quinceañera* on her next egg, big white dress, crown, and all. "I can't wait to turn fifteen and have *my quinceañera,*" she said, spinning it to show me.

"Nice," I said. "The party was fun, but I don't care about a *quinceañera.*"

Lucy said, "You're crazy," as she added a big pink cake to the egg.

Next I drew the weird panty-hose baby doll Mama had made us using her old pairs of stockings.

After about an hour, Papa popped his head out the screen door. We were only starting on the third carton and fading fast. He laughed. "Keep going, you still have seventeen cartons left to go."

Ages later he appeared with a cold pitcher of lemonade, a big cheese quesadilla cut into triangles like a pizza, and a chocolate bar. We perked up.

Lucy and I glowed, showing him the cats and birds we'd drawn, the funny faces, and the strange and psychedelic designs. We even showed him the carton of the weak, wounded, and dead: the eggs we'd cracked or broken altogether.

"Don't worry," he said. "We can still save them. Wait and see." He brought out his old guitar and serenaded us with his favorite song, "*De Colores*," as Lucy and I drank lemonade and devoured the quesadilla and chocolate. His brown and white boots kept time.

"De colores, de colores se visten los campos
En la primavera. . . .

Y por eso los grandes amores de muchos colores me
gustan a mí."

Papa rested his guitar on his lap and pointed to the cartons. "Fifteen to go!" My fingers were throbbing from holding the crayons too hard. And to think I had wanted even more eggs.

Papa said, "I have a surprise." He reached inside the paper bag and took out a pink box with a picture of a yellow chick and a rabbit. The rabbit was coloring a giant Easter egg with a small paintbrush.

We went into the kitchen, where he set eight Styrofoam cups on the table. He poured water into each one, and then a spoonful of white vinegar. He opened the box and took out eight colored tablets. We took turns choosing: I got red, green, purple, and yellow. Papa said, "Drop one tablet into each cup."

I felt a jolt of joy as the green tablet fizzed and sizzled and filled the cup with a cloud of emerald green. The red tablet dazzled with its deep ruby explosion. The other cups held yellow, blue, pink, orange, purple, and violet. Magic.

Papa helped us carry the cups out to the porch, handed us each a spoon, and then showed us how to color fifteen boxes of eggshells in the blink of an eye.

The next day, he brought out a plastic bag filled with round paper jewels of all colors, called confetti. He filled each egg by feeding the confetti through the little hole on top.

Now, with paper jewels scattered over the porch—and us—Papa said, "You can each take one of the eggs and fill it with anything you want, so long as it won't hurt anyone."

As he began to cut circles from a thick roll of yellow crepe paper, I picked up the egg with Berta's face and big teeth on it. The day before, Berta had shouted, "We're still the winners! Twenty-one cartons!"

Lucy and I ran off to fill our special eggs with something secret. I sneaked into the kitchen, opened the cabinet under the sink, and filled my egg with flour. Back on the porch, Lucy grinned and hid hers behind her back.

There were more than a hundred yellow circles of crepe paper as big as half-dollars scattered around Papa. As Lucy and I coaxed each other to reveal what we had put in our secret eggs, Papa went inside and returned with a big bowl of thick white goo. "This is Mexican paste, flour and water. Now we'll paste the crowns on the eggs."

He took one of my emerald eggs and dipped a finger into the goo. He rubbed it around the little hole, took one of the yellow paper circles, and put it over the top of the hole. Then he pressed the edges of the paper circle onto the egg.

He held up the green egg with its bright yellow crown. He shook it, making the confetti rattle inside. "Now you do it."

Lucy and I sat there for hours, until the sun finally set. By then we were not only streaked and colored from the previous day's crayons and dyes and markers, but also covered with confetti and bits of crepe paper and gobs of goo. But we were experts at transforming empty white eggs into magical *cascarones*.

After I had endured the long Easter Mass wearing a white cardboard hat with an elastic around my chin, and after I had traveled miles and miles in the car holding my

Easter basket filled with a chocolate bunny and candy Easter eggs just screaming to be eaten, we finally got to the park near Falcon Dam.

Lucy and I tore out of the car and met up with all our friends and relatives, including Berta, who now claimed to have won with a total of *twenty-five* cartons of eggs. Our fathers barbecued colossal cuts of meat and rings of thick, spicy sausages on silver coals of mesquite. The mothers talked and took walks, admiring the wildflowers, the birds, the big blue sky.

I told Berta, "All your cartons are disqualified since you didn't even bother to color them."

She shot back, "You have too many broken ones." Then Lucy spotted a tiny brown bunny under a bush, so we all started chasing it, trying to claim it as our pet.

After the meal, when we were stuffed with candy, it was time for the *cascarones*.

While we closed our eyes and turned our backs, the grown-ups hid the eggs. I prayed I would find the most of all.

When we heard the whistle, I popped my eyes open, empty Easter basket in hand.

The landscape was completely covered with *cascarones*, as though they had fallen like rain from the sky, sprinkling trees, bushes, and the ground.

After we all scurried around collecting, we ran wild, smashing the *cascarones* on each other's heads. The fathers and mothers took eggs and smashed them too.

It was a riot of laughter and paper jewels and bits of

bright eggshells flying and falling everywhere and on everyone.

Then I snuck up behind Berta and smashed my secret egg *hard* on the very top of her even harder head. Her bewildered face turned completely white with a big *poof* of flour. She growled, bared her teeth, and let me have it with *her* secret egg—filled with thick yellow mustard.

As I kicked the air and swiped at the yellow gobs on my hair, face, and stinging eyes, I could hear Berta's big fat laugh.

Then—*silence!*

There was Berta with real egg running down her hair and face, mixing with the flour. She was spitting and glaring at someone.

I turned to see Lucy smiling from ear to ear, no longer holding her secret egg.

As we drove home, I turned to Lucy.

"Berta must smell like one big fat rotten egg."

Mama laughed. "I finally had to pour a bottle of Clorox down the kitchen sink to kill the smell you caused by putting those twelve perfectly good eggs down the drain."

Papa smiled into the rearview mirror. "And remember, Sofia, your little sister won the competition with Berta for you at the end, and with just *one* egg."

I beamed at Lucy, feeling so, so lucky to have her on my side.

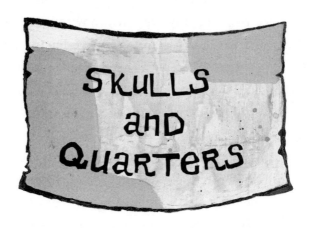

SKULLS AND QUARTERS

"**This**" time I want to go as a *curandera*," I told Mama.

"Why don't you go as a witch instead?"

"But I thought a *curandera was* a witch."

"A *curandera* isn't a *bruja*, exactly," she said, "but someone special who heals others by praying to saints and using herbs. Dressing up as a *curandera* for Halloween . . . well, it just isn't right." Mama picked up her old broom and started sweeping.

I had been dreaming about going as a *curandera* for Halloween since one had come to our house that summer.

She came because Lucy had gotten hit by a car and the doctors couldn't seem to cure her. They didn't find any broken bones, or even cuts, but there was still something wrong with her. She'd scream at leaves blowing on the ground, calling them spiders. She'd burst out crying and say the strangest things, like the time she said she'd swallowed the straight pins she'd seen in a box, when she hadn't at all.

Mama summoned her circle of *comadres*. They gathered in the living room, prayed a rosary, and then, while eating *pan dulce* and drinking cup after cup of hot coffee, they decided that Lucy was suffering from *"susto,"* shock, something no ordinary doctor could cure. Only a good *curandera* could do that!

Then each *comadre* reviewed her solar system of friends and family to find the best *curandera* in their universe.

That's when I heard the name Belia. Not only had Belia done the usual stuff—like curing cases of evil eye with the secret power of a chicken egg, or curing earaches by inserting and then igniting paper cones inside throbbing ears—but she had brought a dead baby back to life just by blowing into it. She had given a poor woman who couldn't have children so many teas to drink and so many saints to bury that the woman wound up with three babies, and all of them with bright orange hair.

That day I asked Mama, "What's a *curandera,* exactly?"

She thought for a moment. "She's like a good witch, someone with a *don,* a gift for healing others through her magic powers."

"Will she be coming on a broom with a black cat?" I asked. But the *comadres* called Mama back into the living room before I found out.

The witch Belia just walked in through the front door. The biggest surprise was that Belia turned out to be Berta's mom. But she did look different, all dressed in black, and serious. I remembered Clara's story where she said that certain *brujas* can turn themselves into wild animals, like mountain lions and eagles. *So the witch Belia turns herself into Berta's mom,* I thought.

I hid behind a door and watched as Belia took a white sheet and draped it over Lucy, covering her from head to toe on her bed. Lucy looked like a dead body.

Belia grabbed the old broom, hairballs and all, and started sweeping Lucy, up and down, up and down, the full length of her body. And as she did, she called out: "Lucy! Lucy! Where are you? Where are you?"

Lucy had been told to respond: "I'm here! I'm here!" This back-and-forth went on and on for what seemed like hours. And then Belia put the broom down, uncovered my sister, and left.

I jumped from behind the door and grabbed the broom. Laughing, I told Lucy, "Do the same thing again, but this time with me."

Lucy giggled and covered herself with the white sheet.

I started sweeping her up and down, calling and asking where she was. "I'm here!" she said.

We were having great fun until Mama walked in with the witch right behind her. "Belia forgot her purse," Mama said, shaking her head.

I froze, broom in midair. Belia would surely put a hex on me now. But she started laughing and said, "Sofia is going to grow up to be a good *curandera!*"

Lucy did get well in a couple of days. And I took all the credit.

That Halloween I agreed to go as a regular *bruja*. I helped make a big witch's hat from a cardboard box, slipped into one of Mama's old black dresses, and allowed her to paint a big black wart at the end of my nose. Poor Lucy had to stay home with the flu.

I loved Halloween even more than Christmas, because it allowed me to be something new. The year before, I'd gone as a big walking tequila worm. Mama had created this crazy costume using yards and yards of plastic she'd borrowed from Tía Petra, my godmother. I crinkled and sweated with every step. The year before that I went as a bean taco. Mama made that even crazier costume from a brown jumper and beige blanket she'd bought for seventy-five cents at Johnson's *Ropa Usada,* the biggest second-hand clothing store *anywhere.*

Mama was always inventing funny things, like her panty-hose baby. But Halloween, like the full moon, brought out the wackiest in her. Poor Lucy had to go as a rainbow *raspa* the year before, sporting a hairy wig that Mama dyed every color in creation. Lucy could hardly walk, all taped up in a giant cardboard cone.

What I liked best about Halloween was candy.

The year before, Berta had told me that she'd gone to the other side of town and found Halloween heaven, where she got whole chocolate candy bars and quarters. I didn't believe her, of course. But then she opened her bag and showed me. It was *amazing!*

I started in the barrio. I got a small skull with my name on it at the yellow house, a cucumber at the pink one, and then a big sugar tortilla at the green one.

At the next house, a white-haired *viejita* suddenly popped out and started drenching me with water, saying, "I hate ghosts, devils, and witches visiting my house! A bucket of holy water should take care of you!"

I ran to the sidewalk where Mama was waiting for me. Something flew over my head. I looked down and found a card with an image of the Guardian Angel attached to an old black boot. Mama picked up the boot, slipped the card off, and dropped it into my bag. She left the crazy *viejita's* boot by her door.

After that it was more cucumbers, carrots, sugar tortillas, pennies, peanuts, popcorn balls, and even a brown egg from a woman with her very own chicken coop, which Mama volunteered to carry. There were flowers, too—fresh, paper, and plastic. One woman asked if I wanted a bean taco.

I did get a couple of lollipops, even one with a tequila worm inside, as well as a few pieces of hard candy, but my Halloween bag was only getting heavier and heavier with vegetables. And I hated vegetables—*all* of them, but *especially* cucumbers.

I stopped. "Mama, I want to go home. Now."

"Why? Why do you look so sad?"

I hesitated. "Well . . . I was hoping to get chocolate bars and quarters. Last year Berta got chocolate candy bars and quarters on the other side of town."

The next thing I knew I was in the car. When we crossed the railroad tracks and came to a stop sign, I looked out and saw princesses, pirates, and penguins in the most amazing store-bought costumes. They were carrying big orange plastic pumpkins for their treats.

And when I came to the first house, a white brick mansion, I pushed a lit-up button and heard bells. The enormous door with the gold handle swung open, and a woman in pointy high heels came out carrying a huge bowl full of Hershey bars and silver-wrapped chocolate

Kisses. I couldn't believe my eyes! I felt the incredible warmth of the big fireplace inside.

I stood staring, forgetting to say "Trick or treat." The woman smiled and dropped a chocolate bar into my paper bag, then a quarter, and then a whole handful of Kisses.

And it was the same at the other five mansions we visited.

When we got home, I put my treats from the other side of town into a second bag, leaving the sugar tortillas and carrots and cucumbers in the first one. And when Lucy asked for some candy, I showed her the first bag.

The next day, Mama told me to come with her to Doña Virginia's. I saw that her house was the same one that had given me the sugar skull with my name on it. We went inside and found Don Chuy, her husband, who took us to a tiny back room. There we found Doña Virginia under a pyramid of covers, her eyes closed, and hardly breathing.

Mama opened her purse and took out her plastic bottle of holy water. She poured some holy water on her fingers and then made the sign of the cross on Doña Virginia's pale forehead.

Don Chuy quietly asked us to come to the kitchen for tea, which he made by boiling leaves from his orange tree. He brought a plate of white skulls to the table.

"These are Virginia's sugar skulls," he said sadly. "She

got up really early yesterday morning to make a big batch of them. She wanted to make sure she had enough for all the barrio kids.

"I insisted she go back to bed, that she was too sick. I said I'd go to the store and buy a bag of candy, of chocolate, even. But no, she wanted to give the kids something connected to the Day of the Dead.

"October thirty-first is so hard for both of us . . . her, especially. Our son Luis would've been Sofia's age by now.

"Sofia, do you know that the souls of children get divine permission to come visit their families on October thirty-first? The adults come on November first. And then they all depart again on November second for another year."

I shook my head.

Don Chuy touched my head and told us how Doña Virginia had dragged herself around the kitchen, making *pan de polvo* and hot Mexican chocolate for Luis and a pot of *pozole* for her parents. Don Chuy took us to their tiny living room and showed us a makeshift altar in the corner, with two flickering votive candles, orange marigolds in a dime-store vase, and small statues of the Virgin of Guadalupe and other saints.

Don Chuy pointed to some black-and-white photos. "This is my son Luis. Those are Virginia's parents." He lifted the lid off a ceramic bowl. I smelled the chilies and pork in the *pozole* Doña Virginia had cooked for her parents. There was a cup of hot chocolate and a plate full of sparkling *pan de polvo* cookies for Luis. *His* favorite treat.

I also noticed a red wooden top, a small stuffed bear, a bottle of tequila, and a cigar, as well as a glass of water, a cross made from lime peel, and a salt shaker on the altar.

Walking home, I asked Mama about the altar and the things I had seen there. She said that Doña Virginia's son Luis and her parents were coming to visit for just one day. The lime cross was to direct them home, the salt to purify them, and the water for them to drink along their way. And once they got home, they would feast on their favorite foods and drinks.

When we got home, I found Papa at the kitchen table reading *Don Quixote.* Lucy was fast asleep.

"Ah, *mi'ja,* show me your Halloween candy," he said, smiling. I went and got the bags from under my bed.

"Why do you have two bags?"

"One has the stuff I got around here; the other has the candy bars and quarters from the other side of town."

The next thing I knew I was back in the car, but this time with Papa. "I'm taking you to the *cemetery* to show you something magical about *this side.*"

The cemetery was strangely aglow with lit candles and sprinkled with orange marigolds. I felt fear, not magic.

"Papa, I don't want to get out of the car."

"Look," he said.

In the cemetery, people were talking, dancing, and playing guitars and singing to the tombs and eating from plates piled high with tamales and other foods. Had some of these people come out of their graves? Maybe Doña Virginia's son Luis and her parents were now over at her house visiting. I thought about the sugar skull she'd made for me—the one with my name on it.

Papa smiled at me and started the car.

"I wish we lived on the other side of town," I said, looking out the window at the darkness.

"Why, *mi'ja*?"

"Because they live in nice houses, and they're warm."

"Ah, but there's warmth on this side too."

"But . . . it's really cold at home, and most of the houses around us are falling apart."

"Yes, but we have our music, our foods, our traditions. And the warm hearts of our families. Remember how the *comadres* all got together and found a way to cure Lucy, and with just an old broom? And it was something those rich doctors couldn't do."

Sometimes I thought Papa was from another world, especially when he talked like this.

"Don't worry, *mi'ja*," he said as he stopped the car in front of the house. "You'll see what I'm talking about as you get older."

I walked into our cold house, nodding and shivering.

TACO HEAD

MAMA used to pack two bean tacos for my school lunch each day. Every morning she'd get up at five to make a fresh batch of flour *masa*. She'd roll out and cook one tortilla at a time until she had a big stack of them, nice and hot, and then she'd fill each with beans that she'd fried in bacon grease and flavored with chopped onion in her huge cast-iron skillet.

And each morning I would sit at the kitchen table and say, "Mama, can I please have some lunch money too, or a sandwich instead?" But the reply was always the same: "Why, *mi'ja*? You already have these delicious bean tacos to eat."

It wasn't that the tacos weren't good; it was that some kids called all Mexican Americans beaners, so the last thing I needed was to stand out like a big stupid sign. All the other kids either bought their lunch at the cafeteria or took nice white sandwiches.

I started going to the very end of the cafeteria, to turn my back and gobble up my tacos.

Then I started eating each taco by first putting it in a bag.

It would take me all of five minutes to eat, and then I'd go outside to the playground. I was *always* the first one there, often the only one for quite a while. But I didn't mind, except on really cold days, when I wished I were still inside.

On one cold day, I so dreaded going outside that I started eating my second taco rather slowly. "Hey, you!" someone shouted. I turned and found a big girl standing right smack in front of me, her arms crossed over her chest like bullet belts.

"What's in that paper bag?" She glared and poked at the bag with her fat finger.

I was stunned stupid. She grabbed the bag.

"Taco head! Taco head!" She yelled. In seconds I was surrounded by kids chanting "Taco head! Taco head!"

I wanted the ground to open up and swallow me whole. Not only was I found out, but the girl had caused my taco to fly open and splatter all over my white sweater.

This nightmare went on forever, until Coach Clarke,

the girls' PE teacher, blew her whistle and ordered everyone back to their seats.

"Sofia," she said, "don't pay attention to them. They're just being mean and silly." She took me to the teachers' lounge and helped me clean up.

For two days after that, I went directly to the playground and didn't eat my lunch until I got home after school. And then for two days after *that*, I ate inside a stall in the girls' restroom.

The next Monday, Coach Clarke stopped me in the hall. "Sofia, how about we eat lunch together in the cafeteria?"

When the lunch bell rang, I found Coach Clarke sitting in the middle of the cafeteria, with students standing all around her. She looked up and waved me over.

"Here, Sofia," she said as she pulled out the chair beside her. "Everyone else was begging to sit with me, but I said no, that I was saving this chair for you."

I sat down, feeling sick, nervous.

"How about we trade?" Coach said. She opened her lunch bag and pulled out a half-sandwich wrapped in plastic. "I'll trade this for one of your tacos."

All the kids were staring at us.

"Oh, please, I really want to trade."

I hesitated and pulled out my lunch. I unwrapped the foil.

"Those look good," Coach said, reaching for a taco. "Better than any stupid sandwich I've ever had. See for yourself. Take a bite."

I carefully unwrapped the half-sandwich and took a little bite. It was *awful*, something between sardines and bologna.

"Ha! Told you!" Coach Clarke said, laughing. "Here," she said, taking the rest of the sandwich, "you don't have to eat it. Have your taco instead."

As I ate one and Coach Clarke ate the other, she kept making all these loud *mmmmm* sounds. I knew everyone in the cafeteria could hear.

And the next day we ate lunch together in the middle of the cafeteria. We traded. Again, her half-sandwich was truly awful. *Do all sandwiches taste like something between sardines and bologna?* I wondered.

But this time, as she ate one taco and I the other, she told me stories about herself: about how she became a coach because she'd fallen in love with sports at school; how she loved playing soccer most but had also been good at playing field hockey and softball. We laughed when she described the funny skirt she had worn playing field hockey.

I told her I liked to play soccer too, with my father and cousins in the street. Then I remembered Clara and her stories, so I told Coach Clarke about Clara and how she told me that I had inherited my great-great-grandmother's gift for kicking like a mule. I hesitated, then said, "I wish I'd kicked the girl who made fun of me."

"Sofia, learn to kick with your head instead."

"Like in soccer?"

"No, like with your brain. And you know how you can really kick that girl, and really hard?"

"How?"

"By kicking her butt at school, by beating her in English, math, everything—even sports."

Coach Clarke and I had lunch together the rest of that week. She asked me for the recipe for the tacos. I had to ask both Papa and Mama for this, since Papa cleaned and cooked the beans before Mama fried them.

After that, I wanted to "kick that girl" so bad that I asked Coach Clarke if I could go to the library to study after lunch instead of wasting time on the playground. She arranged it for me. She also told me, "Part of 'kicking that girl' is to eat your tacos proudly, and right in the middle of the cafeteria."

That year I kicked that girl in all classes and sports, especially soccer.

It wasn't long after my lunches with Coach Clarke that some of the other Mexican American kids started eating their foods out in the open too. And sometimes when I pulled out my lunch, I got offers to trade for sandwiches. But I always ate both my tacos before heading off to the library.

The Fancy School

MRS. West was reading to my ninth-grade English class when a boy from the office walked in and handed her a note. She glanced at it and then looked straight at me. As she started toward me, I froze.

Mrs. West handed me the note. "Go see Mr. Thomas." Mr. Thomas was the school counselor. "Take your books. You might be gone for a while."

What did I do wrong?

As I headed down the hall, I started panicking. *Someone died!* No, no. I prayed now that I *had* somehow gotten into big trouble.

"Good morning, Sofia," said Mr. Thomas, waving me to the chair in front of his desk. "I have some exciting news. A doctor is funding scholarships to send four Mexican American students from the Lower Rio Grande Valley to Saint Luke's Episcopal School in Austin. His own kids are there. It's a terrific school.

"Since you're at the top of your class, I want to recommend you. You'll still have to go through tests and interviews. But I think you have a *great* chance. And going to such a good school will open many doors for you."

He handed me a brochure.

On the front was a picture of a beautiful white stone chapel on top of a hill. It was all aglow. The photo must've been taken around Christmas, for the chapel was surrounded by hundreds of lighted *luminarios,* and another photo showed the inside, decorated with red poinsettias and tiny twinkling lights. What did it mean to go to an Episcopal school? Were the chapel services anything like Catholic Mass?

Inside the brochure, I saw that the school buildings were made from the same white stone and that they surrounded the chapel in the shape of a rectangle, like a fortress. The playing fields were beautiful and green. Thoughts of running down those fields, kicking a soccer ball, filled my head. *No more street soccer.* And there was a girls' soccer team too, with crimson uniforms. *Wow!*

The images of the school seemed like a dream. They made me think of the mansions on the other side of town, where the lawyers and doctors lived. When I read that all the students there graduated and went on to college, I thought of Coach Clarke and learning to kick with my head.

"So what do you think?" said Mr. Thomas, breaking my trance.

"Eh . . . how far is Austin from here?"

"Oh, about three hundred and fifty miles."

"Oh." *So far away!*

"But it's a boarding school, so if you get in, you'll be living in a dorm with the other students."

Silence.

"But you'll be able to come home for the holidays, and for summer."

I wanted to play soccer on those beautiful playing fields. I wanted to get better at kicking with my head so I could go to college. I could get a good job and make enough money to buy a nice house for my parents and Lucy.

But to go and *live* at a school? *Without my family?*

"Sofia, do you think that's too far away?"

"Well . . . my parents . . . you know . . . ," I said.

"Yes, of course. It can be especially hard for the parents, having their child go away to school. But it's a terrific school, and you have already gotten to the very top of what we can offer here. It *would* be a great opportunity to challenge yourself."

Silence.

"So let me suggest this: go talk this over with your family, show them the brochure, and then come see me again next Wednesday at ten. Okay?"

I talked to Berta first, on the porch.

"Sofia, you're crazy! You're the best at everything here. Why not stay, graduate as the McAllen valedictorian, and get a full scholarship to college? Just look at these pictures," Berta said, punching the brochure with her finger. "These are *rich* kids. Snooty. With parents who went to college and all. You might even flunk out!"

"I know, but . . ."

"But *what*? We're fourteen. We should be planning our *quinceañeras*. And here you are planning . . . your, what, your escape!"

"I'm not trying to escape."

"Austin is nine hundred miles away!"

"It's only three hundred and fifty."

"That's *far*, Sofia, *really far*! It's not like you can still live at home and board a bus every morning. . . ."

"I know, Berta."

Silence.

"And what about your papa, mama, and Lucy . . . and *me*?"

Silence.

"Sofia, tell me something: *why* do you really want to go?"

"I just . . . want to see what's out there. . . ."

"But what's wrong with *here*?"

"Nothing. But the Valley is not the whole world. . . . I just want to see what's out there."

"Do you want to go to the moon, too? I mean . . . and here I was looking forward to planning our *quinceañeras*."

"Berta, I *don't want* a *quinceañera*. I love it here, but what I want is to go see new things. I want to go to college, make money, and buy a nice house for Papa and Mama. And maybe become a . . . lawyer."

"A *lawyer*? Women aren't lawyers, Sofia. And especially not Mexican women. They're wives, mothers, and if they're lucky, teachers or nurses. But you can try marrying a lawyer, if you only start dressing better."

The porch door flew open and out jumped Lucy. I stuffed the brochure into my shirt pocket.

"What are you two talking about?" Lucy said.

"Nothing," I said. Berta and I took off.

I waited until the *sobremesa* that evening to bring it up with Papa and Mama. *Sobremesa* was the time right after everyone had finished eating supper and was relaxing and sipping coffee or hot chocolate around the kitchen table. Papa and Mama took turns presiding over each *sobremesa*. Papa said it was a sacred time, like Jesus's last supper, and that it was when we reconnected as a family.

There were only two rules for a *sobremesa*. One was

that everyone had to take a turn and say something. The other was that you had to pay attention, listen to the person talking, and never, *never* interrupt.

Papa was presiding that evening, and Lucy went first. I knew it wasn't going to be easy keeping the second rule when Lucy glared at me across the table and then turned red. She went on and on about how I had been talking to Berta out on the porch before supper and about how we were looking at some secret paper, but when she had come out to the porch, I had immediately crumpled it up and stuffed it into my pocket. And when she had asked what I was talking to Berta about, I had said "Nothing" and run away.

"Sofia, is this true?" Papa said, looking straight at me. I looked down. It was going to be even harder to tell them now.

"So, tell us about this secret?" Papa looked concerned and confused. "This is not like you, Sofia."

"Yeah! Tell her to show us her secret paper," Lucy said.

"Lucy, remember. You can't interrupt," Papa said.

I let out a long, heavy sigh and then took the crumpled brochure out of my pocket. I laid it on the table and tried to smooth it out. Papa took it and looked at it.

"Why is this such a big secret? It's just a brochure for some school in Austin," he said. He handed it to Lucy. "Okay, Sofia, it's now your turn to talk. You know the rules," Papa said.

Silence.

"Yes, and when you talk, I want to hear *all* about whatever you shared with Berta but refused to share with your own little sister," Mama said.

I took a deep breath and told them about being summoned by Mr. Thomas, about the scholarship, the school. I showed them the pictures of the chapel, the playing fields, told them how everyone there went on to college . . .

"But it's in *Austin*," Mama said.

"It's a boarding school, Mama," I said. "If I win the scholarship, I'll live there, in a dorm."

Silence.

"But I'll come home for the holidays and summer."

"I was just starting to talk to my *comadres* about planning your *quinceañera*," Mama said.

"I don't want a *quinceañera*. I don't want to dance around wearing a big silly dress, and—"

"That's *not* what a *quinceañera* is about!" Mama said. "It's about growing up, about learning to act like a *comadre*, and about finally learning to use your *don* to help yourself, your family, your community."

"You mean you want me to grow up to be a *curandera*?" I said, suddenly remembering what Tía Belia had said years before.

"Ah, I think it's my turn now," Papa said, scratching his head. "Sofia, remember your two bags of Halloween candy years ago? And how I took you to the cemetery? Do you remember what you saw there? People were having a *sobremesa* of sorts with their visiting dead relatives. Do you remember this? And do you remember what you said on our way home that night, that you wished we lived on the other side of town because they lived in nice warm houses?"

I nodded.

"*Mi'ja,* do you *really* want to go away to this school, even if it means leaving your home here?"

I sat looking at the table.

I nodded again.

Silence.

"Can you please tell us why?" Papa said.

I shrugged. Part of me so wanted to go on this new adventure. But I also felt frightened. One of the pictures showed the students all dressed up, sitting down for formal dinner. I didn't have clothes like that, and there were so many forks and spoons and knives by each plate. It would be like going to another world. The world of rich people.

"You want to go see what's out there, on the other side? Don't you?"

I nodded.

Mama spoke up. "But what about this side, your family, your barrio?"

Silence.

"Sofia," Papa said, "do you remember what I also told you on the way home that night, about family, tradition? And how your mama cured Lucy of *susto* by getting all her *comadres* together, and how that was something the rich doctors from the other side couldn't do?"

I nodded.

"Your mama and I want you to be happy, to always be happy. And for you to be happy, you need to *learn how* to be happy. Learning to be a good *comadre* is at the heart of this."

"It's now *my* turn at the *sobremesa*," Mama said. "Sofia, your papa is right. So all I can say for now is that we need to have many more *sobremesas* to discuss this. You also need to go talk to your godmother. And *I* need to talk to all my friends.

"But, Sofia, I know *this:* this is really scary stuff. For us especially. You're still young, and your papa and I don't know very much about this other world. So you need to figure out *why* you want to go there."

I nodded.

Mama then looked at Lucy. Papa was looking at Lucy too. Lucy was staring at the brochure. She looked up at me. "I want to go too," she said.

I wanted to hold her, somehow missing her already.

I knew that leaving Lucy would be the hardest and scariest part of all. My parents were grown up and so would always feel connected to me. They knew how to connect even with the dead. But Lucy was still a kid. We had never been parted.

The thought of leaving her made me feel so lonely. As lonely as she would be without me. Still, I wanted to go. And it was then that I felt that somehow I was no longer a child.

MY PLASTIC Tía

T he father of Marcos, a ninth grader from McAllen, drove us all the way to Harlingen. We went into a huge cement building and sat through hours and hours of scholarship tests with about twenty others.

Papa, Mama, Lucy, Berta, and I had been discussing the school for weeks. But early on, we had at least agreed that I should go ahead with the testing.

I was summoned to Mr. Thomas's office a month later. "Sofia, this is Mr. Weld from Saint Luke's," said Mr. Thomas, smiling. Then Mr. Thomas excused himself.

"Hello, Sofia," said Mr. Weld, shaking my hand. He

motioned me to sit next to him. He had neatly combed brown hair, little wire glasses, a crimson tie, and a dark sports jacket with patches on the elbows. I couldn't help thinking that a hunting dog, a beagle, perhaps, would go perfectly with his outfit.

"Sofia, you did very well on the tests. Congratulations!" Mr. Weld said.

"Oh . . . thank you." I didn't even know the results were back.

"And congratulations on being at the top of your class!"

"Thank you."

"What are your favorite subjects?"

"English . . . and math."

"And how many students are in these classes?"

"Thirty or so."

"The classes at Saint Luke's have ten. The tenth-grade class next year, your class, will only have fifty students. And we make sure they all go on to college. Sofia, do you want to go on to college?"

"Yes."

"How about sports? Do you like sports?"

"Yes." *Is this the interview? Everything is happening too fast!*

"So what's your favorite sport?"

"Soccer."

"Saint Luke's has a terrific girls' soccer team. It travels all around, competing with other teams."

I smiled brightly.

"Sofia, I'm here to offer you a scholarship to Saint Luke's Episcopal School." Mr. Weld beamed.

"Eh . . . thank you," I said, feeling my face turning white with shock.

"Are you interested? We'd love for you to come. And Mr. Thomas is so excited."

"It sounds great, but . . . well . . . my parents . . ."

"Yes, of course. I'd really like to meet them, Sofia. I can tell them about the school and answer their questions. I also brought a whole carousel of slides to show them. How about I come over to your house tomorrow, around six?"

"I'll talk to my parents, but how much money will it cost to go to Saint Luke's?"

Mr. Weld lit up again. "The scholarship covers everything. All your family will be asked to contribute is four hundred dollars. A very small portion of the boarding cost."

Four hundred dollars! That's a lot.

My parents received Mr. Weld the next day in the living room with a pot of coffee and a platter of *pan dulce*. Lucy, Berta, and I sat on the sofa and listened to Mr. Weld congratulate my parents on my winning one of the scholarships. I had decided to let him tell them. Papa and Mama smiled politely at Mr. Weld and then looked at me. Berta and Lucy jabbed me in the ribs.

Mr. Weld projected his carousel of slides onto the wall

with Mama's five flying angels. Mama offered to take them down, but he said, "Oh, no, Mrs. Casas, they bring magic to my show." Berta and I laughed. And the slide show *was* magical. Especially the images of the emerald green playing fields.

After Mr. Weld left, Papa, Mama, Lucy, and even Berta seemed subdued, while I was excited. "Hey," I said as I placed my hand on Lucy's small shoulder, "who died?"

Silence.

"*Mi'ja,*" Papa said, "we're very proud of you, that you won one of the scholarships. Right, Mama?" He stood up.

"Eh . . . yes, *mi'ja*, we are," Mama said. "But . . . well, we still have to decide—as a family—what's best for you. Whether you should accept it. So it's time for you to go see Tía Petra."

Lucy and Berta didn't say a word.

The sofa—covered in plastic. The lamp shades—covered in plastic. The coffee table, the dining room table, the everything table, even the carpet—plastic, wall-to-wall plastic, strips and strips all taped together. Tía Petra's house had everything wrapped and lined, covered and trapped in plastic. That was how it was on the day I went over to see what she thought about the scholarship, since Tía Petra was also my godmother.

I found Tía Petra carrying a fat spool of tape.

"I'm not rich," she said as she pulled out more and more of her sticky tape to cover something, "but my things will last forever—and will always stay brand-new, too."

She sat, swallowed up in her enormous wine red armchair, moving one bare thigh this way and that way because her sweat had pasted her to the plastic. She pried her arms from the armrests, making a rude sucking sound. I sat on the massive matching sofa, not knowing if and how and when to move, but ever more concerned that the pools of sweat gathering around my thighs and legs would soon start running like rivers onto her plastic-covered carpet. Every two minutes or so I turned to pull up the purple octopus doily—yes, one of Mama's wacky creations—that kept sliding down and bunching on my neck like a big ball.

I wanted to yell, *Why don't you just go ahead and enjoy your furniture? Uncover it!* But she would say, "I understand how to keep things new, how to keep things lasting forever, truly a great secret." Recently, she'd even arranged for the funeral home to line her entire casket with plastic, so that she didn't ever have to worry about bugs or dirt or anything.

Tía Petra left and then returned with a plate of hot, crispy cinnamon-covered *buñelos*. They smelled so good. I took the top one. "Tía," I said, "can I eat it on the sofa?"

"*No!* That'll dirty the cover. Come to the table. I'll get you a plate." And of course, the table was entirely covered with . . .

I pulled out the school brochure. Tía Petra returned

with a plate and a big glass pitcher of bright red hibiscus water. She poured me a glass and then sat down beside me. I thanked her, took a sip, and then handed her the brochure. "It's a school in Austin. I just won a scholarship to go there."

"Yes, your mama told me. I'm so proud of you, *mi'ja*. This is for when?"

"For next year . . . if I get to go."

"Do you want to go?"

"Yes."

"What about your papa and mama?"

"They're still talking about it. We've already had a million *sobremesas* on it."

"*Ay, mi'ja,*" Tía Petra said laughing. "It's always harder on the parents. And then there's little Lucy. But let me tell you a secret. I'm your godmother, right?"

"Yes."

"Do you also know the secret of the godmother?"

"Well . . . you sponsored my baptism . . . and you're supposed to take care of me . . . if something ever happens to my parents."

"Yes, that's all true. But as your godmother, I also have a say regarding your education. Did you know that?"

"No."

"Yes, but here's the catch. Your education means not only your school and book education but your spiritual education as well. Do you know what I'm talking about?"

"Is it about learning to be a good *comadre*?"

"Yes, of sorts. So your papa and mama have mentioned this?"

"Well . . . sort of. In a way that makes them sound like they're from another world."

Tía Petra started laughing. "What do you mean?"

"Well, Mama worries that if I go away to Saint Luke's, I won't learn to be a good *comadre*. And when I asked what that meant, Papa said that it was at the heart of learning to be happy."

"*Ay*. Two Martians talking. That's because you're still young, Sofia, and learning what your mama means takes time. And not through books but through experience, and having *comadres* around to help you."

"But I'm happy now, so why do they keep saying they want me to learn to be happy? They also talk about discovering my *don* and things like that."

"Yes. I'm glad you're happy, Sofia. But like I said, you're still young. When I was your age, I was happy too, and thought I would always be that way. And no one could tell me *anything*. But as I got older, well, things got trickier. And then my father died. That's when things really got hard. Part of learning to become a good *comadre* is learning how to feel happiness, especially after life gets tricky.

"But now I'm talking like a Martian too. So let me stop. Now *you* tell me all about this school and why you want to go there. As your godmother, I'll then see whether I think this is good for your education or not."

Tía Petra kept pouring me glass after glass of hibiscus water as I went on and on about the school.

We heard a loud knock on the door, and in walked Mama, Papa, Lucy, and Berta.

They sat down at the table and Tía Petra brought in more *buñuelos* and a new pitcher. As everyone helped themselves, Tía Petra sat down at the head of the table and cleared her throat. She said how proud she was to have me as her godchild and how seriously she took her duty of overseeing my education, how impressed she was by Saint Luke's, and how wonderful it was that I'd won one of the scholarships.

She took a loud drink and said that I had promised her that I would work just as hard at learning to become a good *comadre* as I would at my school studies and that I would write her every week from Austin, and she agreed to monitor my progress carefully.

Pow! I hit my glass with my elbow. All five of us shot up, frantically grabbed the sides of the tablecloth, and jiggled it this way and that, trying to keep the red river from pouring onto the plastic-covered carpet.

After cleaning up every last drop, Tía Petra stood up, smiled, and said, "My secret has done its magic again!"

She left the room and returned carrying a roll of plastic, scissors, and a big spool of tape. "Sofia, come here," she said. She whispered, "*Mi'ja,* trust me. Don't move."

She wrapped the plastic all around me and then took the tape and sealed me into it like one giant bean taco.

Everyone started laughing, especially Lucy. "Yeah! She's always spilling stuff," Lucy cried. "She should go around like that!"

I couldn't believe it. And Tía had even asked me to *trust* her.

But Tía Petra came and stood right beside me. She cleared her throat and then pointed at me. "*Compadre, comadre,* Lucy, and Berta," she said, looking directly at my parents. "Yes! Believe in plastic. But you can't keep Sofia sealed up. Let her go, if that's her dream. And I promise you, as her godmother, that I'll help tutor her on everything she needs to know about her life here." Tía Petra leaned over and yanked the plastic off.

Before we left she presented me with a secret box. Inside, I found a Bic pen and a plastic-covered spiral notebook. My name was written in bold black letters on the front, and right below, LESSONS ON BECOMING A GOOD COMADRE, in even bigger ones. "That's for your weekly letters to me," she said, and she gave me her blessing by laying her warm hand on top of my head and then closing her eyes for a second of silence.

As we stood on the porch, Tía Petra said, "Wait. I want to talk to Berta and Sofia alone for a minute." Mama, Papa, and Lucy kissed her goodnight and went to wait in the car.

"Berta, I'm your godmother too, right?"

"Yes, Tía."

"Well, I want you to help Sofia with her goal of going to that school."

Silence.

"Berta, Sofia needs you. She needs you to be her very first *comadre*."

"*Ay,* Tía, . . . but . . ."

"But what, *mi'ja?*"

"I don't know if *I* want Sofia to go. It's so far away."

"But it'll be good training for both of you. It'll teach you how to stay connected from afar. And when you get good at this, it'll be easier for you to learn to stay *comadres* with the dead."

"With the *dead?* Tía, you're joking, right?"

"No, Berta. Being a *comadre* is never a joke. This is why you must *always* choose them carefully. A true *comadre* is forever."

Silence.

"So will you be Sofia's first one?"

"But what do I have to do?"

"Support her dreams, that's all. And hers is to go to that school."

"But what if it's a big mistake?"

"It's still her dream. She'll figure that out herself. And if it's a mistake, it's her mistake, and she'll have to learn from *that*. Won't you, Sofia?"

"Yes," I said.

"But remember, Sofia, a *comadre* is always free to tell you what she thinks, like it or not."

"Okay."

"Yes, I think this will be *very* good training for both of you. So, Berta, will you do it?"

"Well, I guess so . . . yes."

"And you, Sofia, will you be Berta's first *comadre*, too?"

"Yes, of course, but I don't know what her dream is. . . ."

Tía Petra laughed. "Oh, Bertita will have *too* many along *her* way. Just wait and see. That's the secret behind those great teeth of hers. She'll always be biting off more than she can chew."

I laughed, and eventually Berta did too. We kissed Tía Petra goodnight.

When we joined Papa, Mama, and Lucy in Papa's old Ford, Berta said, "Sofia, I'm . . . so, so . . . excited for you, really." They stared at Berta.

"Eh . . . thanks, Berta," I said, smiling. "Yes, thank you *very much.*"

As we drove home that night and I stared out at the passing darkness, I felt I had never loved Berta more.

CLeaning Beans

EVERY Tuesday Papa would come home from the cabinet shop where he worked, change into his jeans and boots, and then take the yellow metal container from the kitchen cabinet. He would sit at the kitchen table, take the lid off, and start cleaning his pound of pinto beans. I would always join him.

It was a Tuesday, and I now only had a couple of weeks to decide whether to accept the scholarship. As I sat down beside Papa and watched him clean his pinto beans, I wondered what it would take to finally convince my family to let me go. Tía Petra's plastic performance and Berta's support had surely helped my cause, but I still hadn't gotten the blessing from my parents.

Papa dipped his left hand into the metal container and fished out a fistful of beans. He raised his hand to his chest and opened it. Using his index finger, he began looking through his little mountain, a gentle giant. As he pulled out pebbles, clumps of dirt, and broken beans, he put them in the upturned lid. He also kept blowing on them as he poured them from hand to hand like jewels. This helped clean off the dirt.

After turning and moving all the beans around, making sure they were now clean and none were broken—broken ones only got stuck to the side of the pot and burned—he slowly spilled his handful into a big brown clay bowl.

That was how he cleaned his pound of pinto beans every Tuesday—handful by handful. He said that holding and cleaning them relaxed him, made every single one meaningful—sacred, even.

I loved sitting and cleaning beans with Papa. He told me secrets about beans, how they were better than meat, how they were like us, mestizo—the pale part Spanish and the brown spots pure Indian.

He'd often pick up a single one, squint at it, and ask me whether I saw the image of Pancho Villa in the scattering of the Indian spots, or Zapata, or the Mexican comic Cantinflas, or my Tía Petra or this or that. I always looked but never saw anything. Still, I said that I did. It was better than watching stars, he'd say. Watching beans was a lot like watching a Mexican channel on TV—*only* Mexican things came out.

But usually we cleaned in total silence. And that was when I felt especially close to Papa. He was the only person I knew who made me feel I could be perfectly quiet and still enjoy something really warm and special with someone.

After the bowl was half full, Papa filled it with fresh water and started moving the beans around and around with his long, golden-brown fingers. He liked the sound, like the waves at Padre Island.

When the water turned gray, Papa drained it all off and washed the beans again, until the water stayed completely clear. Then he poured the beans into the big clay pot. The pot was brown, with a red rooster on its belly. This was Papa's only prized possession, and it was solely used for cooking beans. It was the only pan or pot that had its own space in the kitchen—on the right back burner of our old gas stove.

He then poured in fresh water, put the pot back on the stove, and lit the burner. He watched it until the water started boiling.

After exactly two minutes, he turned the burner off, picked up his old guitar, and came and sat beside me. While we waited for a whole hour to pass, Papa taught me some new chords on the guitar, and we listened to Coco, Papa's yellow canary, singing outside. This hour, he said, cleaned the beans of their wind-making powers, which always made me laugh.

Then Papa rinsed the beans once more.

Now it was time to cook. Papa poured in fresh water, added a sprig of *epazote*, a green plant that awakened the true taste (another bean secret), and lit the fire under the pot.

Once the pot started to simmer and bubble, Papa started bubbling too. The smell was the earth's incense, he said as he took a deep whiff. He then started his bean dance, continuously prancing up to the bubbling pot, lifting its lid, and peeking inside.

Later, he spooned two beans out of the pot and pressed each between his fingers, testing them. "These are better than any piece of meat or steak."

Once the beans were perfect, Papa spooned a cup for me and one for him, and we sat quietly at the kitchen table enjoying them, one by little one, using tiny spoons. This was when beans tasted best, we both agreed, when they were whole and still hot from just being cleaned and cooked.

Now the front door slammed and in burst Mama and Lucy. Lucy was sucking noisily on an enormous lollipop, the colors of a rainbow. Mama dumped two big grocery bags on the kitchen table and flipped the radio on.

"*Ay!*" She cranked up the radio. "It's like a funeral parlor in here. You two should go outside and do something, *anything*. How you two can just sit there for hours without saying a single word. . . . And Sofia, you should be more like Berta. We saw her out shopping for stockings. She's already planning her *quinceañera*."

"Julia," the *vals* sung by Javier Solis, started to play. "*Ay!* That's our song, *viejo!*" Mama said as she pulled Papa out of his chair.

Lucy and I stared. I hadn't realized Papa could dance. He was waltzing Mama around the kitchen, beaming at her. Mama was laughing, her head back, her hair flowing. They looked like teenagers.

When the *vals* ended, Mama planted a big smack on Papa's lips. This made him turn bright red. He laughed, took Mama's right hand, and kissed it gently. "*Gracias, mi amor.* It's an honor to dance with such a beautiful woman."

"Girls, that was our wedding song," Mama said as she emptied the bags. We all started to help. She took out a bottle of cooking oil, a white onion, two serrano chilies, and her big cast-iron skillet.

After she diced the onion and the chilies, she put the skillet on the stove and poured a stream of oil into it. "It's a complete mystery to me how you two can eat those beans right out of the pot. As far as I'm concerned, they're not even cooked yet. You need to transform them into re-fried beans." Mama tossed the onion and chilies into the hot oil.

Papa and I watched as she scooped cup after cup of beans from the pot, poured them into the sizzling skillet, and mashed them with her big green-handled wire masher. "This is dinner tonight," she said, and began to make flour tortillas, using the *masa* she'd made early that morning.

Mama left Papa and me in charge of cooking dinner. Papa picked up the pot and showed me that not one of our beans had survived. They were bubbling away in Mama's skillet. "Next time, Sofia, we'll be smart and save a secret portion just for us. But we need to be quick, before your mama gets to them."

I laughed. One of the flour tortillas started blowing up like a giant bullfrog. "Flip it," Papa said, smiling.

I grabbed the edge, but it was way too hot. Papa reached over my shoulder and flipped it. "Be careful, *mi'ja*. Try using a fork."

"But you and Mama use your fingers."

"Ah, but that's because we have a lot of experience. You're just starting out."

I laughed. "That sounds a lot like learning to become a good *comadre*.

"Papa, there are only a couple of weeks left. They'll give the scholarship to someone else if I don't accept it."

"Ah," Papa said as he lowered the flame under the bubbling skillet. "So tell me, Sofia, what's the difference between how we like to eat our pinto beans and your mama's?"

"Oh, that's easy. We like them whole, eaten from a cup, whereas Mama likes to smash them, fry them, and then trap them into tacos."

Papa laughed. "What? You don't like your mama's tacos?"

"Yes, I do. But they once got me called Taco Head at school."

"Taco Head?"

I told him the story.

"That must've been hard for you, *mi'ja*. But don't tell your mama, because she'll grab her machete and go after that big girl."

"It happened years ago."

"Oh that's a mere detail when it comes to your mama. Your mama's a *huracán*, a force of nature. You've seen her use her powerful solar system of *comadres*."

"Yes . . . but I'm nothing like her."

"No, you're like your papa. But don't feel bad. We have our own secret powers. We find God among the pots and pans, just like Teresa of Ávila, our little Spanish saint."

"Pots and pans?"

"Do you remember those fireflies years ago? How we caught a bunch of them and squashed them all over our faces, arms, and necks? Your mama said, *How could you get so dirty? And those poor creatures!*"

"But then we stepped outside into the dark night, re-member? How amazed and enchanted she was then, for there we were, glowing like some supernatural beings."

"Yes . . . but . . ."

"And take your Taco Head story too, the one you just told me. It must've been really, really hard for you. But look where it's taken you. It kicked you to the very top of your class, and now you have this scholarship."

"Papa, do you want me to go? Can I go?"

"I want you to be happy, *mi'ja*, to learn what it takes to always have the ability to make yourself happy."

"*This* will make me happy."

Papa looked down at his brown and white boots and then at me. "Okay, Sofia. And know that I want you to al-ways follow your dreams. You're a dreamer, like me. And I see from your Taco Head story that you have the kick it takes to learn from life, to keep on going, even when it gets hard."

I kissed Papa. He smiled.

"But what about Mama, and Lucy?" I said, flipping a blown-up tortilla with a fork.

Papa started laughing. "To your mama, the beans aren't done until they're refried. And Lucy is a mini ver-sion of her." Papa turned off the burner.

"That's another important lesson of learning to be happy, Sofia, of becoming a good *comadre*—realizing that everyone is special and often quite different from you. And that if you really want to connect with them, to love them, you need to first figure out how *they* feel. Take me, for instance. I had to learn to *dance,* something I had no interest in, just to have a chance at getting to know your mama. And that's because she *loved* dancing and dances and everything to do with them."

"But . . ."

"But you're all confused now. Well, that's good too!"

"Good?"

"Yes, good, Sofia, because life is like that—confusing. And it's confusing because people are confusing. But *basta!* with all this talk from another world, as you like to say.

"Sofia, seriously, as your papa, let me say this: if this is your dream, to go to this school, I'll support you. Now, on the other hand, you still need to convince your mama. As for Lucy, she'll go along with your mama."

"But how?"

"By learning to dance, just like I did."

"Are you serious? Papa, that's . . ."

Papa started laughing again as he took the last tortilla off the griddle and put it inside the ceramic tortilla holder. "You have to connect with her in a way she can feel and understand, in a way that takes care of her, too. That's what I mean when I say you need to learn to dance. Your mama is a dancer, not a dreamer like you and me. She needs to see and hear things; she can't sense things in silence, like we can.

"Let me give you an example. Remember that Sunday years ago when you panicked and put the host in your shirt pocket, and how your mama called the priest?"

"Yes," I said. Such a strange memory!

"Well, your mama came into the kitchen carrying your shirt and told me what was in the pocket. I laughed and told her not to worry, that I would simply tell you a magic story about how we could now use your secret host to keep angels hovering all over the house."

"Angels?"

"Yes. You know how they tell you that a whole horde of heavenly angels come down right when the priest starts transforming the host into Jesus's body. And how they fly around all during Communion, making sure not one single host gets lost along the way.

"The way I saw it, if we kept your little host in your pocket, then we'd automatically have all these angels hovering over our house. I told your mama that this story would make you feel better, and fast.

"But I sensed that she really felt she had to call the priest. And I knew that this would work out for you, too.

"It must've been scary for you to have to go talk to the priest, but if I hadn't agreed to calling him, your mama would still be panic-stricken about having a now-moldy holy host in the closet.

"Sofia, do you see what I'm saying?"

"But what can I possibly do or say to take care of her so she won't mind me going away?"

"Well, try this: tell her you love her, and that you can take care of yourself."

"But she knows I love her. . . ."

"Sofia, like I said, she's not like us. She only feels what she sees and hears and—"

Mama stomped into the kitchen. "Carmen called to tell me about the great new movie playing at the drive-in, one with Pedro Infante. I'm so excited!"

As Mama took over the kitchen, Papa winked at me. I followed him outside. There was a beautiful orange glow on the horizon. The evening air was sweet with Papa's Mexican jasmine.

"As I was saying, she only feels what she sees and hears, and what she experiences in the movies." He then started to laugh. "So when we go to the drive-in, pay attention to your mama and to how she connects to the movie."

I rolled my eyes. *No, not another one of those singing* charro *movies.*

"So I guess it's time you learn to dance, *mi'ja*." Papa said, smiling. He started whistling the *vals* "Julia." He then took me in his arms and began waltzing me around and around the freshly cut grass.

The Drive-in

i T had been *years* since I'd been to the Border drive-in
theater. According to Mama and Berta, I'd been so fo-
cused on my books that I had missed some of the best
movies ever.

Lucy was sitting between Berta and me in the backseat of our old white Ford, while Noe sat between Papa
and Mama in front. As the car passed the marquee, I
tapped Berta on the shoulder and pointed. We laughed,
for most of the black letters spelling PEDRO INFANTE were
either falling off or missing completely.

After Papa parked on top of one of the rows and rows

of asphalt mounds, it was just like always: Mama leaned over and moved Saint Christopher and the Virgin from the center to the right side of the dashboard. She opened the glove compartment, pulled out a snakelike green coil, set it on top of the dashboard, and lit it. This was incense for killing the flying bugs and mosquitoes. The coil burned with a strange glow that got redder and redder as the evening got darker.

"Mama," said Lucy, "can you please take Saint Christopher and the Virgin off the dashboard? They're blocking my view."

"*Ay*, Lucy, it's always the same thing with you. The movie hasn't even started. And anyway, I'm not taking them off. They're there to sanctify our car and protect us against accidents."

"*Mama*, the car's parked. It's not moving," Lucy said. Berta and I grinned at each other.

"Well, you never know. Something could always happen. Look, I'll move them all the way to the right." Mama carefully set them on the corner of the dashboard.

"Aren't you going to turn them around so they can watch the movie?" I winked at Berta.

Mama turned her two *santos* to face the huge white screen as she always did, and we laughed. I leaned over to Berta and whispered, "I can't wait for the kissing, the tequila drinking, and the shooting to begin. Wonder what Mama's *santos* will think then!" But Berta didn't laugh.

Then Lucy and Noe fought over who got to take the

metal speaker that hung on a pole outside and attach it to their window. Berta and I looked at each other: once we had been the ones fighting over this. Mama grabbed the speaker, hung it over the top of her window, and turned the knobs.

A man's voice burst forth: "Fresh popcorn, cold Cokes, hot dogs, chocolate bars, and pepperoni pizzas are waiting for you at the concession stand!" I used to love going to the concession stand, for there were four magic horses next to it. The horses flew on swings back and forth, back and forth, making me feel as though I were flying through the stars.

"Let's go ride the horses, Sofia!" said Lucy.

"Yeah!" said Noe.

"Okay, let's take them," I said. Berta rolled her eyes and opened her door.

Berta and I tried to keep up with Lucy and Noe. They were leaping and laughing way ahead of us.

"Hey, Berta, what's wrong?" I said.

"Nothing, why?"

"You seem so . . . quiet."

"No. It's just that I'm here to see the movie. This kid stuff bores me."

"You want to *see* the *movie*? Boy, I feel I've missed a lot."

"Yes, you have."

"Like what?"

"Oh . . ."

"Oh, *what?*"

She was silent.

As I watched Lucy and Noe fly away on their magic horses, I noticed that Berta looked older, pretty, and somehow her teeth didn't even look big anymore. They went perfectly with her face now. Her curly, light brown hair was neatly tied back with a red ribbon, and she had on a bright blue dress with glass buttons in front. She was even wearing makeup. *When did all this happen?*

I looked down at my torn jeans, my white T-shirt, my old white sneakers. My hair still looked like Apache hair, as Papa liked to call it—long, dark, and wild.

Then a loud horn blew. Berta told Noe and Lucy to get off the horses—*now!* That she didn't want to miss the movie. Back to the car.

Papa and Mama stayed in the front seat while the four of us took the Mexican blanket from the trunk and spread it on the asphalt mound next to the car.

Just as I thought, it was another one of those singing *charro* movies Mama loved.

But this was our green light to start gobbling whatever we'd brought along with us. Sometimes it was a bucket full of corn on the cob or *Maguacatas,* the boiled pods from our ebony tree, or mesquite beans or bean tacos or *pan dulce.* But this time we felt really, really lucky, for Papa had stopped at Whataburger's and bought hamburgers and Cokes.

After we had finished eating and then made spiral

toys from the paper cups, I looked up at the screen and saw that the *charro* was singing another boring song. I rolled my eyes. But Berta was watching with a dreamy expression.

I couldn't believe it. We *hated* these movies. "I'm going to the car. You all are making way too much noise," Berta said. I laughed but carefully watched as she got into the backseat.

Berta was glued to the movie, just like Mama. Papa smiled and waved at me. He leaned his head against the car door and closed his eyes. I wondered if taking Mama to the movies was another example of his learning to dance.

I joined Lucy and Noe in our usual game of gazing up at the stars and calling out what shapes and animals we could make by connecting them. We also looked for falling stars, sure signs of good luck.

When the *charro* and the *señorita* finally kissed, Lucy, Noe, and I made our usual loud lip-smacking sounds. But Berta was as captivated as Mama. Papa was asleep. And when I coaxed Lucy to go over and ask Mama how Saint Christopher and the Virgin were enjoying this part of the movie, Mama said, "Be quiet." Berta said, "*Shhh!*", not taking her eyes off the screen.

Lucy jumped up. "Restroom time!"

I opened Berta's door and whispered, "Berta, come with us."

Berta sighed. "You all act like a bunch of babies."

We passed car after car and people on aluminum

chairs, milk crates, or blankets. I also saw two sofas and even a church pew. Some young couples were kissing as the *charro*'s song and the *señorita*'s sighs floated over everything.

I looked at the mile-long rays of light shooting from the top of the concession stand, magically painting the movie onto the screen. "Remember, Berta, how we wished we were twenty feet tall, so we could project shadow puppets onto that enormous screen? Especially during the kissing."

Berta just looked at me and frowned, making us walk faster and faster, constantly turning around to watch the screen. "You're all acting silly and ruining the movie for me," she said. Noe and Lucy made even louder kissing noises.

I studied Berta as we walked, thinking about what Mama had said while Papa and I were cleaning beans, that I should start being more like Berta.

Berta turned and bared her now perfect teeth at me. "Sofia, what are you looking at?"

Once there, Lucy and Noe pretended to use the restroom and then begged to ride the flying horses again. I smiled, knowing they had learned this trick from me. But Berta said, "No!" We headed back.

Berta jumped into the car, while the three of us went back to watching stars. I leaned back on the blanket, folded my hands under my head, and stared up at the darkness.

I glanced at the screen. Now the *charro* and the *señorita* were married with children. But instead of the movie, I saw Mr. Weld's slides of Saint Luke's projected onto the screen. *Who are those rich people anyway?*

I turned to the stars and now saw them as faraway worlds. *Yes!* That's what I wanted: I didn't want to stay a kid, but I didn't want to enter Mama and Berta's grown-up world either—at least, not so fast. And not if it was only about getting married and having children, like in the movies. No, I wanted to explore.

I spotted a falling star. I kept it a secret. It was good luck! Yes! *But what if it's a sign of crashing and burning?*

As we dropped Berta and Noe off at their front porch, I remembered what Tía Petra told us on *her* porch. When I got home, I called Berta.

"Sorry we ruined the movie for you."

Silence.

"Listen," I continued, "is there something I don't know? . . . I mean, remember what Tía Petra told us . . . about being *comadres* and all."

"Sofia, it's late."

"I know it's late, but . . ."

"Well . . . I have . . . a boyfriend."

"A boyfriend? Wow! Who is it?"

Silence.

"Why is this such a big secret?"

Silence.

"Jamie."

"Jamie, the track star?"

"Yes."

"Have you kissed him?"

"*Sofia!*"

"I'm just kidding, Berta. I'm not as immature as you think. I'm *worse!* No, no, I'm really happy for you. And again, sorry for ruining the movie. *Now* I understand. "And Berta, one more thing. How do you want me to support this new dream of yours?"

"Actually, I'm glad you asked because I was going to come over to tell you tomorrow. Now good night."

"Good night."

As I drifted off to sleep, I realized that staying happy did get tricky, just as Tía Petra had said.

And I hadn't even left home.

Berta's Quinceañera

The next morning I was sitting at the kitchen table looking at the school brochure and thinking about the picture of the students all dressed up for dinner. I was also thinking that even if I got Mama's blessing, how could I raise that four hundred dollars, the "parents' contribution"?

Berta walked in the door, all excited. "Sofia! What are you doing?" She grabbed the brochure. "Boy! I don't know. You're such a tomboy, and look here," she said, pointing to the dinner picture. "All the girls are in nice dresses. You can't even bother to comb that crazy Indian hair of yours."

I grabbed it back.

"No, seriously. You're the smartest person I know, but you still look and act like a kid. Why don't you grow up?" Berta walked over to the counter and poured herself a cup of coffee.

I sighed. I wanted to just laugh it off, but I stared blankly at the table, knowing that Berta was leaning against the counter, staring at me.

"Okay," I said. "Let's not start this again. You said you were coming over to tell me how I can support your dream. So tell me."

Berta sat down at the table. "I want you to be my *dama de honor*, my maid of honor at my *quinceañera*."

"What do I have to do exactly?"

"Well, you're going to have to look and act mature, for one."

"Come on. Tell me or I won't do it."

"Oh! But I've already talked to your mama months ago."

"And what does *she* have to do with this?"

"A lot. She's one of the *comadres* who's helping me. And she thinks this will be good training for *you*."

"For *me*?"

"Yes! It will help you, especially since you told her you don't want a *quinceañera* yourself. As my *dama de honor*, you'll have to wear a long dress, have a *chambelan*, and dance at my ball."

"I don't have a long dress or a boyfriend, and I don't know how to dance."

"The *comadres* have taken care of all that. You think I'd leave these things to you? *Dios mio!* Look, you're my best friend and this is my party, and—"

"Okay! Okay!" I said. "I'll do it. But remember, you told Tía Petra you'd support my dream. Papa said I can go to that school, but I still need to convince Mama."

Berta smiled. "Okay, it's a deal: you be my *dama* and I'll help convince your mama. But you'll see the two are connected. And you know what?"

"What?"

"After the *comadres* are all done with you, you'll know that you're not only smart, but pretty, too."

I sighed. But now I was at the point where I'd do *anything* to go to Saint Luke's.

The next seven days were pure hell.

We drove around and around in Berta's new car—a bottle green Chevy, her parents' birthday present. Berta had a special "hardship license" to drive at fifteen since Tía Belia didn't drive, her brother, Beto, didn't live at home, and her papa had an injured foot.

We drove from the bakery to the flower shop to the dress boutique to the church to the caterer and then back to the bakery. How could *any* of this possibly have anything to do with connecting with Mama?

After triple-checking on the cake, I got into the car and kicked the seat. Berta started backing out. "Is this it?

I mean, we've already stopped everywhere at least twice. I hope we're heading home now. I really need to study."

"No! Sofia! Remember? I told you that I needed you until *eight* o'clock tonight."

"But for *what?*"

"Now we're going straight to La Plaza hotel."

"But we were there yesterday!"

Berta started laughing.

"*What?*"

"You'll see." As Berta stepped on the gas, I noticed she was wearing new white sandals and *stockings*. I looked at my torn white sneakers. I started to get a headache.

"Oh, Sofia! Cheer up! It's not that bad. *Is it?*" At the traffic light, Berta turned and smiled with her perfect white teeth. I shook my head and kicked the seat again.

"Sofia, what are you thinking?"

I shook my head.

"What?"

"*Nothing!*" I sighed.

"*Sofia!*" Berta, said, driving again. "Stop being a mule and talk to me. I can't read minds, you know."

"How is this all going to help me connect with Mama? I don't have much time left."

"Okay, *genius,* here's a clue: why do you think I'm having a *quinceañera* in the first place?"

"Because you've turned fifteen."

"*Wrong!* Sofia. It's because the *comadres* are making it happen for me. They all got together, including your mama, and they have been helping me plan it for at least six months now. And they're making it really special and beautiful.

"My family alone could never have done this. For one, they wouldn't be able to afford it. And two, a *quinceañera* is my coming-out party, yes, but it also brings everyone together. So, all in all, it's helping me learn how to be a *comadre*."

"*How?*"

"Well, I had to learn how to go about getting *padrinos* and *madrinas* to sponsor and pay for my cake, the dance, the flowers, and on and on. I also had to assemble my court of honor by finding fourteen *damas* and fourteen *chambelanes* to represent my past fourteen years. I had to go talk to the priest about the spiritual meaning of turning fifteen.

"It's like preparing for your First Communion. It's all about growing up and joining the community."

Berta turned left onto Main Street.

"As for your mama, start acting like you're not a kid anymore, and show her that you can take care of yourself."

"But *how?*"

"Sofia, I know you can look out for yourself. Your papa knows too. But to your mama, you're still a kid. And no mother is going to send her kid away, especially to a world she doesn't know. So you need to *show* her that you've grown up." Berta parked the car. "Show her that you can function in the real world too, in the world of people, not just in your books and soccer and those crazy stories you tell. And you can start doing it right now!"

"What do you mean?"

"It's a surprise!" she said.

Berta dragged me through the massive door of the hotel, the most beautiful in the valley. It was white stucco with a red-tiled roof and tiled floors and secret courtyards and stone fountains like a Spanish hacienda.

Berta walked me out to the main courtyard. "Sofia! Sofia!" It was Mama. "Hurry! You only have ten minutes before it starts!" I turned and saw Berta laughing from across the courtyard. She was standing with Jamie beside the Spanish fountain.

As I followed Mama to the ladies' room, I got a few clues as to what this *surprise* was about. One was seeing Berta's other *damas* standing around in their new dresses. Tía Belia, who was a seamstress, had been busy making them. Mama was carrying a big paper bag with her.

Then I bumped into Beto, Berta's older brother, in a tux! He had terrific teeth like Berta, and he was over six feet tall. He flashed a big smile at me. "Sofia, are you ready to dance?"

I laughed. My headache was back. "She will be!" Mama said as she hurried me along. "Beto's your *chambelan*," she said as we passed the twelve mariachis tuning their instruments. They looked dazzling in their black charro outfits, with silver buttons all down their pants and vests.

"Here." She took my dress out of the bag.

I went inside one of the stalls and put it on. It was white, with orange and green lace trim along the waist and collar, and puffy sleeves.

"Sofia! Come on out! You're late!"

I sighed, then remembered what Berta had said. I put on a smile. But my headache kept getting worse.

"Oh! Sofia!" Mama said. "You look so pretty, so *grown-up!*"

Wow! This is working!

"Thank you, Mama," I said, tripping.

"Hold still," she scolded. I stood stiffly, doing my best to keep my smile going, as Mama pinned a pair of earrings on me, then added her pearl necklace, a touch of lipstick, rouge. But I drew the line at stockings. I put on my flat black shoes.

"Oh! It's amazing!" Mama said as she came at me again with a big tube of red lipstick. "You're so beautiful!"

I started rolling my eyes but caught myself and smiled instead. "Thank you, Mama." My headache had spread to the very front of my head.

For the next three hours, Berta's royal court was put though an excruciating hands-on crash course on the correct use of utensils, polite conversation, handling social "mishaps," and dancing.

This boot camp culminated with our having to go out

to the courtyard and dance to the *vals* "*Dulce Quinceañera.*" As I inadvertently kicked Beto in the shins for the fourth time, I wondered why the boys always got to lead.

❦

That night I found Papa at the kitchen table carving something with his knife, and I told him what the *comadres* had just put us through.

"Ah! La Plaza hotel. That's where I first saw your Mama. She was dancing in that very courtyard. And that's when I fell in love with her."

It was hard to imagine Papa falling in love, for he was always so calm, reserved, thoughtful; falling in love sounded like losing control.

"Yes, back then, La Plaza held a dance every Saturday. I went one Saturday with a couple of friends. I had just returned from the Korean War. We were out in the courtyard, drinking beers. The mariachis were playing. Couples were dancing. And then I saw your mama dancing a *vals.* She was wearing a bright red dress and had the brightest smile, the sweetest eyes. She looked *so beautiful.*

"I stood there watching her all evening. Of course everybody wanted to dance with her. And she did every kind of dance—*rancheras,* polkas, *cumbias, valses.* She was *amazing!*

"But I realized I didn't stand a chance with her unless I could dance too. Now it's your turn to learn."

We went outside and Papa taught me how to dance the lead to "Julia."

On Berta's big day, I woke early and made breakfast for everybody. Then I put on my dress and let Mama pretty me up.

The priest's blessing of Berta at the church was followed by the reception. And after Berta had posed for a zillion pictures, the *damas* all danced with her. Then Berta's father started waltzing her around the courtyard.

Berta's mother appeared carrying a white satin pillow with a tiara and high heels. She placed the pillow in front of Berta, and then she and Berta's father replaced Berta's flower headpiece with the tiara and her flat shoes with heels.

The *vals* started again, but now Berta danced with all fourteen of her *chambelans,* and finally with Jamie. She looked so beautiful in her flowing white dress, and so grown-up. It struck me how much I'd miss her if I went away to school. How much I'd miss all my family and friends!

Finally, Berta's towering cake was wheeled into the middle of the courtyard. Her parents reached up and took the little doll from the top of the cake, a replica of Berta—tiara, gown, and all. They presented it to Berta as her last doll ever. Berta cut the cake.

Later in the evening, Papa whispered something to

the lead mariachi. Papa looked so handsome in his dark suit and his brown and white boots. Then "Julia" started to play. He whispered to me, and I walked across the courtyard.

"Mama, can I have this dance?" I said.

She looked surprised and then laughed as I took her in my arms and we started waltzing, just like Papa had taught me.

"Mama," I said, counting steps in my head, "I love you."

"I love you too, *mi'ja*. It's like a dream. Me and you dancing to 'Julia,' in the same courtyard where I met your papa. And you looking so beautiful, so grown-up."

"Mama, I have a dream too."

"What's that, *mi'ja*?"

"To go to that school."

"What does Papa say?"

"He supports it, so long as you do."

"But what about Lucy?"

"*Ay*, Mama, she's just like you. She'll go along with whatever you say."

"But what about those dresses you'll need, and the four hundred dollars?"

"Don't worry about that. My *comadre* Berta and I got all that figured out."

"Your *comadre* Berta?" Mama laughed. "Okay, *mi'ja*, you have my blessing." Mama had tears in her eyes.

We kissed when the *vals* ended. As we sat at the table, I winked at Papa and turned to Lucy next to me.

"Lucy, is it all right if I go to that school? Mama and Papa say it's okay, if it's okay with you." Lucy looked at Mama, who nodded.

"Okay," said Lucy quietly. I moved closer and squeezed her hand. "I'll come home as often as I can," I whispered.

"So let's celebrate!" Papa said. "I'll be right back." He returned with Berta in one arm and a tiny bottle of mescal in the other.

"Sofia!" Berta beamed. "I told you our dreams were connected."

Papa poured five *copitas* of mescal. Mine was a drop.

"To Berta's and Sofia's dreams!" Papa said, toasting. He gulped his down. I gulped. Coughed. *Whoa!* Everyone else took a sip.

"And, Sofia, always remember Clara's cure for homesickness—the tequila worm." Papa fished the worm out, dangled it between his fingers, then bit it. He started chewing it, *slowly*.

"Yuck!" we all said.

"Sofia, here's your half," Papa said. "I left the best part for you—the head. And remember to chew it slowly. It won't dissolve like a holy host."

Yuck!

"Berta, want a big bite?" I said.

"No way!"

I took the head of the tequila worm. *Squishy.* I put it

in my mouth. *Squishy.* And started chewing. It felt . . . I swallowed. *Squishy.*

"Gross, Sofia!" Everyone laughed.

"And," Papa said, "once you go, I'll be sure to send you a whole tequila worm in the mail." I laughed, but anxiety flooded me.

I'd been so intent on getting my parents to let me go that I hadn't thought about actually leaving.

Five "New" Dresses

The phone rang early the next morning. Berta. "I can't believe you ate the tequila worm. *Gross!* How did it taste?"

"Terrific! But it didn't cure my problems."

"A tequila worm cures homesickness, not problems."

"Well, I've got two big ones."

"What are they?"

"How to get those five new dresses and the four hundred dollars," I said. "I told Mama that you and I had a plan. I even called you my *comadre*."

Berta laughed. "You're quick, Sofia. Let me come over

and show you the *quinceañera* pictures. Then we can talk and talk about a plan like real *comadres*."

"You mean your *zillions* of pictures are back already?"

"Yeah, and I made extras of you and your mama dancing!"

"And how many did you make of you and Jamie kissing? A *zillion*?"

"*Two* zillion!"

The most daunting thing about going to Saint Luke's was not that it was over three hundred miles away, or that it was Episcopalian, not Catholic, or even that it was way up on a hill, away from anything and everything. No. It was having to dress up every evening—Monday through Friday—for a formal sit-down dinner.

This had worried Mama, too: "So even if we decide that you can go, Sofia, what are we going to do about your clothes? You only have one decent dress—the one you wear to Mass." I thought of the piggy bank Papa bought me years ago in Mexico. It contained about three dollars, not enough for even *one* dress.

I kept having the same nightmare over and over again: I was sitting down to dinner in my Sunday dress, and there were seven other students at the table, which was set with the finest silver, china, and crystal. They all stood up and started pointing and laughing at me. I looked down and was horrified to find that my nice white dress had turned into one taped together with pieces of Tía Petra's rolls of plastic. I woke up in a sweat, remembering "Taco Head!"

Mama and Lucy were visiting the *abuelitos* across town. Papa was on the front porch, watering his Mexican jasmine and listening to his singing canary. I made a fresh pot of coffee and was putting out a plate of pumpkin empanadas when Berta came into the kitchen carrying two huge photo albums and a big bag.

"Wow!" I poured coffee. "It'll take us years to—"

"And these are only the really good ones."

After our third cup of coffee and our third empanada, we were only halfway through her pictures. *I'll die if I see one more shot of her kissing Jamie,* I thought.

"Okay!" She slapped the albums shut. "You've done a really good job at being my *comadre* by looking at my pictures. You even got the props down—kitchen table, coffee, *pan dulce.* So now let's talk about *you* and those dresses."

"Not until we talk about you and Jamie. What's it like kissing him?"

"*Sofia!*"

"No, really. It's important that I help you, too. . . . Remember what Tía Petra said."

"My dream is not about kissing Jamie."

"So what is it about?"

"Well . . . it's about being with him, about how he makes me feel about myself."

"And how's that?"

"Like I'm in a dream . . ."

"And kissing him, what's that like?"

"That's . . . *personal*. . . ."

"Come on, Berta. You can't treat me like a kid and tell me to stop being one."

"Umm . . . kissing him is like . . . well, going outside yourself. You feel wobbly and all."

"And you *like* that?"

"It's hard to explain. I don't really understand it either."

"So how do you want me to support all this?"

"Well, you can help me not flunk math. It's hard to study when you're in . . ."

"Love?"

"Sofia . . ."

"Okay, okay. I'll help you with your math."

"Thanks. Now, those dresses . . . Why don't you do what I did with my *quinceañera*? Get yourself some dress *padrinos* and *madrinas* to sponsor and buy them!"

I sat up in my chair. "I can't do that!"

"But why not?"

"Because . . . it's not me. I have to do this my way."

"*Sofia!* What's wrong with getting other people to help you? That's part of learning to be a *comadre*, anyway."

"I know. It's just . . . well . . . It's just like Papa. . . . You know, how he wanted a guitar and then went about making one in his cabinet shop, using his tools and stuff. That's how I am too."

"You're going to make these dresses *yourself*? You can't even button your buttons straight. I told you to take home ec with me, but no! You took advanced algebra."

"I know, but . . ."

"But *what*?"

"Well, you took home ec, so you must know something about sewing, and . . . How about we take my *dama* dress and you help me make it into one of my new dresses?"

"Your *dama* dress?"

"I'll think of you every time I wear it. It'll just hang there in the closet otherwise. *Please,* Berta? "

"But what about the other four?"

"Well . . ."

"Oh! *I* have an idea! I'm bigger than you, right? Remember that blue dress I wore to the drive-in? Do you like it?"

"Yes, it's nice."

"That's dress *two*!"

"What?"

"It's yours. I'll just make it fit you!"

"No! I'm not taking your dress."

"You're not *taking* it. I'm *giving* it to you. It's a present."

"No."

"Yes! Part of being a *comadre* is learning to receive. So we have *two* dresses, and only three to go."

Papa walked in. "Berta, how wonderful you looked at your *quinceañera*!" Berta showed him the picture of me dancing with Mama.

"Ah! My two girls look so beautiful. And that *dama* dress, Sofia, makes you look so grown-up."

I kicked Berta under the table when she blabbed to Papa about our plan for my new dresses.

He took out his thin wallet and pulled out a crisp ten-dollar bill. He handed it to Berta.

"I want to be the proud *padrino* of the third new dress," he said, beaming.

Papa poured himself some coffee. "I have all the faith in the world that you two will conjure up the other two somehow." Then he went outside.

"Sofia, how much money do you have in that tequila worm of yours?"

"About three dollars. Why?"

"That's *perfect!* I've got it all figured out!"

"Figured *what* out?"

"Your other two dresses! How we're getting them! And for only about three dollars!"

I'd heard wrong.

"Maybe even cheaper. On Saturdays everything goes on sale—for thirty cents a pound!"

"A pound? What's selling for thirty cents a pound?"

"Your new dresses!"

"*What?*"

"Yes! We're getting your other two dresses at Johnson's *Ropa Usada.*"

I shot to my feet. "We can't go *there!*"

Johnson's *Ropa Usada* had been a running joke between Berta and me for years now. The name conjured up the whopping shock we'd gotten when we'd first walked into the massive concrete-and-cinder-block warehouse near downtown McAllen. It was a colossal room covered wall to wall with fifteen- to twenty-foot-high mountains of bras, panties, plaid shirts, fuzzy slippers, baseball caps, T-shirts, snow pants, overalls, work gloves, jackets, dresses, boots—everything and anything, even yellowed wedding dresses.

Tiny squealing kids squirmed all over these colorful mountains: rolling down their sides; chasing each other over piles and piles of clothes to where their mothers sat in craters, sifting, piece by piece, through the mounds around them.

Anything the Salvation Army and Goodwill didn't want eventually came here to Johnson's *Ropa Usada* to get picked over one last time before getting shipped off to the Third World. For a flat fee, you could buy a whole bale. They would open it for you and you could choose whatever you wanted inside, leaving the rest to become part of one of the mountains nearby.

So if you bought something here, you also acquired the dubious honor of wearing a shirt or dress that everyone else in the entire country had rejected and cast off, even those who got their clothes at secondhand stores.

The first time we went, Berta and I had laughed so hard we fell into a pile of clothes, tears running down our faces.

"No way!" I said as we parked in front of Johnson's. Berta began to laugh.

"*Berta!*" I said. "You're supposed to be *helping* me. People *died* in those clothes. . . . Everyone will laugh at me." My nightmare came back to me. Taco Head at a formal dinner.

"Don't worry!" Berta said. "When I'm done with them, they'll look tailor-made—perfect. No one will ever know where you got them."

I thought of what Tía Petra had said about Berta: she often bit off more than she could chew.

I left Johnson's *Ropa Usada* carrying a couple of old dresses, a bathrobe, a tangle of neckties, and a king-size bedsheet—all for $2.35. Berta had insisted, "Trust me, Sofia. You'll see. Anyway, you should be *thrilled,* since my mother agreed to help us transform all our stuff. You'll be like Cinderella."

For the next two weeks I spent every afternoon and evening at Berta's house. Under her mother's supervision, Berta measured, cut, and sewed. I helped the best I could, by counting buttons, cutting, and doing anything Berta and her mother asked me to do. But mostly I climbed on and off a chair, to stand and get pins stuck everywhere.

My *dama* dress only needed to be shortened. Berta's blue dress with the glass buttons in front was the second one. The third came from Wal-Mart, bought with Papa's ten dollars. It was bright yellow, with white piping and a smart white belt.

When it was time to work with the bathrobe, the tangle of ties, and the king-size bedsheet from Johnson's, I shuddered as I got onto the chair.

"*Trust me,* Sofia!" Berta kept saying.

Jamie would sometimes stop by for a Coke. That was when I did my best to help Berta with her dream by telling him stories about how smart, kind, wonderful, and pretty Berta was. Then I kept watch for Tía Belia so the two could sneak a kiss or two.

And every night, I helped Berta with her math.

Somehow Berta turned the bathrobe into my fourth dress. It was red cotton with a bow Mama made from the tangle of ties. We laughed long and hard, remembering all of Mama's crazy creations, especially the tequila worm Halloween costume and her panty-hose baby.

"Berta, you've done terrific magic so far, but I'd rather die than be seen wearing a bedsheet to dinner!" I said, as she started tracing a pattern on the king-size sheet.

Berta laughed and just kept on tracing, cutting, pinning, sewing. As she snapped the thread with her perfect teeth, I kicked my foot, worrying.

A few nightmares later, she called.

"Sofia! Your fifth and best new dress is ready!"

She met me at the door with a green dress on a hanger.

Well, it does look *like a dress,* I thought as I put it on. But everyone would instantly know what it was made from!

Mama and Lucy came over to marvel at the five "new" dresses. They insisted I model each one. "The green is by far the prettiest! So elegant!" they all agreed, clapping. It was emerald silk, with a narrow waist, three-quarter sleeves, a rounded neck, and a delicate black Asian design.

Mama thanked Berta and Tía Belia over and over.

"Now, Berta," said Mama. "Has Sofia been a good *comadre* to you, too?"

"Oh! Yes!" said Berta. "I would've flunked math without her." And not gotten to kiss Jamie so much, I added silently.

I smiled at her as she adjusted my belt. Helping her was nothing compared to what she'd done for me.

Lucy looked longingly at us.

The Packing Shed

The door slammed. "It feels strange doing math so early," Berta said, throwing her book on the kitchen table. I measured coffee into the pot. "Please make it extra strong. I have my final tomorrow. God, how I *hate* math. But, Sofia, it doesn't take a math whiz to know that you have a big zero toward that four hundred dollars you still need."

"Yes, I know. But let's get cracking on your math." I sat next to Berta and opened her book.

Berta shut it. "I can't even look at numbers without a ton of coffee. So what are we going to do to get your four hundred dollars?"

"I'll get a job."

"What job? You know how things are around here, with so many people unemployed. And you don't have any experience."

"I know. . . ."

"Why don't we get family and friends to sponsor you, to be your school *padrinos?*"

"That's the same idea you had with the dresses. Papa said he'd take on some extra work. But I told him I want to earn this money myself."

"I'm helping Mom with some sewing projects this summer. You can help, and we'll—"

I started to laugh. "Berta, you're so sweet. No wonder Jamie's crazy about you. *Me,* sew? No, I'll just go downtown and find a job."

"But *how?*"

"I'll just get out there and figure it out."

"Sofia, you *are* a mule. At least let me drive you there."

"I'll be fine." I jumped up. "Coffee's ready! Now open that book."

The next day I woke early, dressed, and then walked toward Main Street in downtown McAllen. Summer had just started but it was already sweltering, with temperatures over a hundred by noon. It was about a three-mile walk.

When I got to Main Street, I dusted off my shoes,

straightened my skirt and my shirt, and double-checked that all my buttons were buttoned straight. I stared at the stores. I had no idea how one went about asking for a job, what I'd say if they asked if I'd ever worked before, or been a saleslady or cashier or anything.

When I opened the glass door to the Popular, a women's dress shop, I froze. Salesladies were buzzing around, waiting on customers. And they all wore makeup and earrings and high heels and stockings. My flat brown shoes and bare legs seemed terribly out of place. Why in the world would any woman want me to wait on her, I thought, much less ask me for any fashion advice?

I walked around in a daze and then pretended to be looking at some blouses. I jumped when I heard a woman's voice behind me, asking if I wanted any help. I mumbled that I was only looking. The next minute, I was out the door.

I walked farther down Main Street. Most of the stores were either dress shops or clothing stores. In Woolworth's, I could see myself unboxing toys, sticking plastic flowers into those green Styrofoam squares, even folding towels. And, maybe, if I was really lucky, they'd let me serve scoops of ice cream and glasses of Coca-Cola at the long red food counter.

"Excuse me. Who do I see . . . to apply for a job?" I finally asked a lady wearing a name tag.

She looked me up and down. "Aren't you a little young? Back there." She pointed. "Go ask for an application."

I took the two long pages and struggled through the application. When I went to hand it in, I was embarrassed by the cross-outs and scribbling in the margins. But I made sure to smile and thank the woman who finally took it.

I spent the next five hours walking into every business on Main Street, even the dress shops, and filling out applications.

But when I started back home, I dragged my feet. I probably wouldn't get a single call. I had absolutely no experience, and the unemployment rate in McAllen was one of the highest in the nation. But if I didn't make the four hundred dollars, I wouldn't be able to go to Saint Luke's.

As I crossed the 18th Street canal and then the railroad tracks, I heard machines. I looked up and saw that I was near the two packing sheds four blocks from my house.

I had always seen and known about the packing sheds, but I had never given them much thought. All I knew was that they were open and busy during the summer picking season. This was when we'd get knocks on the front screen door and find young boys selling bags and bunches of carrots, onions, bell peppers, cantaloupes, cucumbers— whatever extra fruit or vegetables were being cleaned and packed in the packing sheds that day. The rest was boxed, loaded, and shipped on the railroad that ran right in front of the sheds.

I walked to the packing shed and up the wooden stairs. Inside I saw a whole army of well-dressed Mexicans working. Men were operating noisy machines that dumped loads and loads of green cucumbers on a moving conveyor belt. A row of women stood on wooden pallets by the moving belt and tossed the cucumbers into large wooden bins. Another row of women stood on the other side of the belt and packed the cucumbers into white cardboard boxes. Young boys worked at one end of the shed making boxes. Forklifts moved full boxes to the far end of the shed, near the railroad tracks.

How well dressed the workers were: the women wore nice dresses and makeup; the men, good shirts and trousers—even though the shed was dank and dirty, its floors were completely covered with water, and the greasy machines ground away incessantly.

As I stood staring, a man wearing a white hat and shirt and crisp blue jeans walked up to me. He squinted. "Are you looking for a job?"

"Yes!"

He led me to his tiny office and told me to fill out a slip of paper. "Good. You can start working this minute."

The man took me, stunned, to where the women stood in front of the moving conveyor belt. Hundreds upon hundreds of cucumbers kept moving on it. The man said, "Stand on the pallet, just like the women. Your job is to sort the cucumbers into large, medium, and small, by tossing them into one of the three bins on the other side of the belt. Toss the large ones into the first bin, the medium into the second, and the smallest into the third. The women on the other side will pack them into boxes."

I now stood on the wooden pallet, working at my very first job. I didn't feel grown-up and proud, as I thought I would, but completely overwhelmed and panicky, for the cucumbers moved down the conveyor belt like a furious green river. And they all seemed to be about the same size. As I stood before the rushing river, I quickly glanced at the women to my right and to my left. They looked like wild windmills, tossing cucumbers left and right. Slowly, I started to pick and throw one cucumber and then another, still confused about the sizes.

After thirty minutes and then a whole hour, I was tired, and the cucumbers just kept coming faster and faster. When I looked down at the wet floor underneath the pallet, I noticed that the women on each side of me were wearing pumps. How could they manage to stand here all day?

During a ten-minute break, the belt stopped and the women got together and talked. Some of the men went out to smoke. I found a pay phone and called home.

"Papa, I found a job! I'm working at the packing shed down the street—the big one."

"*Ay, mi'ja,* that's really hard work. Come home. I'll find a way to raise the money," Papa said.

"No, Papa, *please.* I want to earn the money myself."

"You're too much like me, *mi'ja.* That's not always a

good thing. Come home. Relax. Spend the summer with Lucy and Berta. Go visit the school."

"I'd rather work, Papa. We have a late shipment, so I'll be late tonight."

I worked until ten o'clock that night. When Papa came to pick me up, I was dizzy and could hardly feel my legs. I climbed into the car and sank into the seat. "Papa, the Mexican workers are all dressed up as if going to church, even though it's so dark and dirty and noisy in there. And we all stand on wooden pallets because the floor is completely covered with water."

The next day Papa came to get me at midnight. Mama was still up when we arrived home, but I was so exhausted that I didn't eat the dinner she'd warmed up for me. I just fell into bed, wearing the wet jeans and T-shirt I'd worn all day.

The days and then the weeks all seemed to blur together into a haze. All I knew was that I'd somehow gotten through the ten- or twelve-hour days. But I also knew that the cucumbers were making me crazy. I dreamed about cucumbers: walls of them falling on top of me as they sprouted faces and screamed at me.

Then they started to attack me during the day. I caught myself squeezing Papa's tube of hair gel onto my toothbrush, or putting the coffeepot inside the refrigerator, and seeing green cucumbers everywhere. I saw them on walls, on faces, even in the sky.

After a month, I stood there at my post, shifting from

one foot to the other and doing my best to sort, when the man with the white hat appeared next to me and said loudly, "If you don't work much, much faster, I'll have to let you go."

He walked back to his tiny office, and the woman to my right leaned over. "Don't worry," she said in Spanish. "He always does this—picks on somebody or other, thinking this will just scare everybody into working even harder." I smiled but kept my eyes on my flying hands. Faster! *Faster!*

At the ten-minute break, I asked her, "How long have you been working here?"

"Five years," she said. "I come from a little village in Mexico, near the border."

I so wanted to ask why she and the others dressed up to come work in this wet and dirty place, but I didn't.

By my last month at the packing shed, I knew I hated cucumbers above anything else in the whole world, and vowed to never, ever eat another one.

But that last month of my first job, I also received my first proposal. I was sitting on the steps during a break, trying to bring my stiff legs back to life, when a young man in a nice pair of black trousers and a long-sleeved white shirt walked up to me. I knew he drove a forklift. He smiled at me and then bowed his head politely. He said, "My name is Miguel. And I think you're really pretty." He paused, cleared his throat, and asked, "Would you be interested in marrying me?"

I shot up and squinted, bewildered. He smiled and repeated, *"Would you be interested in marrying me?"* This time less shyly. I looked down at my faded wet jeans and my torn sneakers.

"I don't even know you."

He shook his head. "The picking season is almost over, and I'm afraid I'll never see you again. That's why I'm proposing to you now, before I have to go back to Mexico."

"I'm just fourteen and haven't even thought of marriage. . . . Actually, I'm going away to school."

"What is your name?"

Just then the break ended—the conveyor belt started moving again—and we returned to our jobs.

I tossed cucumber after cucumber into bins, and I thought I finally understood why they all dressed up in their best. I *needed*—not just wanted—more than this.

When I got home that night, I sat down at the kitchen table.

"I made your favorite dish," Mama said. "Cheese enchiladas!"

"I know, Mama, but I'm just not hungry." I laughed and told her about my first marriage proposal.

"That's *sad,* Sofia." Mama shook her head. "And things are only getting crazier. Young people used to meet in plazas, at dances, at church, under the safe eyes of the community. But now everything is changing so fast. I just heard La Plaza hotel is putting a pool in the courtyard where your papa and I met.

"And I'm especially worried about Lucy, now that you're going away. Things will *really* get crazy by the time *she* grows up."

I nodded. For the first time ever, I detected a sense of fear in Mama, that even her web of *comadres* was no match against these changes. And maybe, I thought, going away to school might help me help her someday.

The Canicula

IT was Sunday, August first, my birthday. And best of all, I didn't have to go to the packing shed today.

We had all just returned from Sunday Mass. Papa was on the porch carving something with his knife. "*Mi'ja,* I'll barbecue some fajitas for your birthday dinner tonight. Invite Berta over."

I called Berta.

"Sofia? Aren't you *boiling*? And it's only ten in the morning!" I laughed, thinking that I was simply so happy not to be working with those crazy cucumbers that I hadn't even noticed the heat.

"How about we drive around in my car, in the air-conditioning?"

"Great!"

Mama walked into the kitchen and started opening all the drawers, then the cupboards.

"What are you looking for?" I said.

"The keys to the cedar chest," she said, opening the stove.

"You're looking in the *stove?*"

"It's the *canicula*," she said as she opened the refrigerator door.

"The *what?*"

"The *canicula.*"

"What's that?" I'd heard the word before.

"The forty days between July fourteenth and August twenty-fourth, which are the hottest days of the year and when the cotton gets picked."

"But what does that have to do with losing your keys?"

"*Everything, mi'ja*, because the craziest things happen during the *canicula*. But to this day, I still don't know whether the *canicula* makes people crazy so they do crazy things, or whether it makes things crazy to make *them* crazy."

"Mama, now, *that's* crazy," I said.

"See, the *canicula* is getting to you, too! Your eyes are rolling like a *loca's*." Lucy and I started helping her look for the keys, sweat dripping down our faces. "Mama, what do you want from the chest?" I asked.

"That's a *secret!*" she said, and then she and Lucy started laughing.

The air conditioner in Papa's Ford had broken down on Monday. He had taken it to the garage, left it there for four hours, and then picked it up. It broke down the very next day. He took it back and they told him that it was the radiator now. They fixed that. But when it broke down for the third time, the garage manager blamed it on the *canicula*, saying that these dog days were killing cars like crazy. I worried whether Papa's Ford would even make it all the way to Austin and back when it finally came time to take me to school.

I kept looking for Mama's keys while Lucy left to buy *pan dulce* at the *panadería.*

She came home with a big bag. She opened it, peered inside, and then frowned.

"What!" she said, taking out gingerbread *cochinito* after *cochinito.*

"Why did you buy so many pigs?" I said.

"That's the thing. I didn't even pick *one.* I picked everyone's favorite *pan dulce.* And look here, fifteen *cochinitos!*"

"The *canicula!*" Mama said. "Don't even bother going back to exchange them."

After Berta found Mama's keys under a carton of eggs on top of the refrigerator, we dropped Mama off at the *abuelitos'* even hotter house, and then Berta, Lucy, and I kept driving around, just to keep cool.

I pointed to a temperature sign flashing 114 degrees. We drove two blocks and I pointed to another, flashing 118 degrees.

"Two blocks and there's a difference of four whole degrees. Is that crazy or what?" I said, now rubbing my eyes and thinking of the green fields at Saint Luke's.

"Do you want to keep driving around or do you want to go to Wal-Mart?" asked Berta as she turned the corner.

"Wal-Mart? We went there last night!"

"Sofia, you know people here don't go to Wal-Mart to buy things. It's an extension of their homes, but with cool air and colorful things to see. And that's where the *comadres* have started going to meet and talk. Like you go to the library for books, they go to Wal-Mart."

"Yeah!" agreed Lucy, suddenly poking her head between Berta and me.

"Well, I'll tell you both what *I* want. Pull over and let me drive."

"You don't even have a driver's license."

"*Berta*, Papa taught me everything. Now, come on. It's my birthday." She shook her head and then pulled over. We switched sides.

Papa had taught me to drive his Ford, but that was a standard. This would be my first try at an automatic. But I had been studying Berta, and it looked like a piece of cake—with only two pedals and just shifting from park to drive, and sometimes reverse. *A piece of cake!*

I turned the ignition on, shifted to D, and then kicked off.

"Not bad," said Berta.

I headed toward the high school, feeling a little sad that I'd never get to go there. Was it smart to be passing up graduating with my class, my friends? What if I *did* crash and burn at Saint Luke's? Was it crazy to take the plunge into an unknown world? Was I being a mule?

Berta started laughing.

"What are you laughing at?" I said as we passed McHi and then the purple and gold water tower with the fierce McHi bulldog painted on it.

"The other day Beto told me about how he used to drive his friends around in that old car of his. And when it was over a hundred degrees outside, right when he caught sight of McHi, he'd give a sharp whistle and everyone would roll up their windows."

"Why?"

"So that people would think they were so cool with the air-conditioner on."

"That jalopy that jerked and cracked like a fire-cracker?"

"The very same one. And you know what?"

"What?"

"Beto told me he thinks you're pretty!" Lucy started making kissing sounds.

"*God*! I'm *so* glad I'm getting away from here and especially from you two *locas!*" I said as I headed down Twenty-third Street toward the church. We could see waves of heat rising up from the hot asphalt like smoke.

"Do you remember your idea, Sofia, of wetting towels and draping them over our legs to keep cool at night?" Berta said.

"*Remember?* Lucy and I still do it. And now that we're *comadres*, Berta, we have to get some of those paper fans that are stapled to those wooden sticks that the doctor uses to choke you, and start fanning ourselves as we gossip and gossip," I said, driving past Navarro School, where Berta and I had gone as kids.

"Can I do that too?" asked Lucy, her head still between Berta and me.

I was going to say something funny or sarcastic, but then I caught a glimpse of Lucy's big bright eyes and realized that she was serious. "Do what?"

"Be a *comadre* with you and Berta?" I looked at Berta and winked.

"Of course," I said, smiling. "And your new *comadres* have a surprise for you."

"What?" Lucy said. She almost climbed into the front with us. Berta looked at me, wondering.

I pulled the car into the church parking grounds and turned it off. I leaned over and whispered into Berta's ear. She smiled. I pulled my seat back. I gently felt the pedals.

"Lucy, come sit with me. You're going to help me drive

Berta around." Lucy beamed. As we went around the church's parking lot for the tenth time, with Lucy at the helm, she lit up more and more.

"She drives *way* better than you!" Berta said.

Then Berta went back to driving, but now with our new *comadre* Lucy sitting between us. Something so simple as letting Lucy steer meant the whole world to her. I had to remember to jot that down in the notebook Tía Petra had given me.

"Hey," said Lucy, "will you and Berta help me plan my *quinceañeara?*"

"You're barely *ten!*" I said.

"Hooray, Lucy!" said Berta. "It's *never* too early to start. *Of course* I'll help you. And here's some important advice: forget getting any help from Sofia on this. She's great at bugs, books, soccer, and crazy things, but—"

"But I want Sofia to be my maid of honor," Lucy said.

"Whatever you want. Do you have a boyfriend too?" I said.

"Maybe I can get Noe to be my boyfriend." Berta and I started laughing.

"Okay," I said, "you work on that. And while I'm away at school, I want you to spend time with your *comadre* planning, and be sure to write me about it."

"Okay. Can we make our *quinceañera* dresses, just like you and Berta made your school dresses?"

"Sure, sure, whatever you want," I said, kissing Lucy's forehead.

"Sofia, when are you planning to pack? You leave soon!" said Berta.

I sighed. "I know. I know." The thought of packing scared me. I just didn't feel ready to go.

When we finally returned to the *abuelitos'* house, we found Mama and Abuelita sitting at the big round kitchen table drinking hot coffee and admiring a blue ceramic whale. "It's for the Christmas *nacimiento* this year," Abuelita said. "And Sofia, you will be the Christmas *madrina.*" It was too hot to pay attention.

"Mama, how can you stand this heat?" I said, opening the freezer door and sticking my head inside. "Do you think it'll ever rain?"

"As a child," Mama said, "I'd stand saints on their heads to try making it rain. But the best thing for keeping cool was getting my father to buy a big block of ice at the ice store. I used the metal ice scraper we bought in Mexico to go back and forth, back and forth on the ice block until I got enough shaved ice for ten *raspas.* For syrup, I used an extra-sweet pitcher of red hibiscus water."

We kissed the *abuelitos* good-bye, got back into Berta's car, and headed to the *raspa* stand on Twenty-third Street.

As we sat outside the stand at a lime green table under a bright blue tarp, the sun slowly began to set. The rainbow *raspa* felt cool and refreshing on my tongue.

"Girls, the *canicula* isn't really that bad, and it's only for forty days," Mama said. "And sitting here, eating an ice-cold *raspa,* watching the sun set, is actually rather nice, especially compared to what the *canicula* meant when I was your age.

"Then, it was being out in the blazing sun, picking cotton. Your papa and I did that for many years growing up."

A young boy dropped his three just-bought cherry *raspas* on the hot pavement. "It's the *canicula,*" I said, and gave him a crisp dollar for new ones—a cucumber dollar I'd earned at the packing shed.

When we got home, we found Papa out in the backyard standing beside his grill. Nobody could beat Papa's fajitas.

Mama went into the kitchen and started conjuring up a stack of flour tortillas and chili salsa. She made a batch of refried beans and saved a bowl of whole beans for Papa and me.

After a glorious fajita feast, Lucy came in carrying a round chocolate cake with fifteen candles blazing. She and Berta had secretly baked it at Berta's house. Papa grabbed his guitar and they all stood around me singing *"Las Mañanitas."* I closed my eyes, made my secret wish, and then blew out all the candles with one big puff.

After the clapping and double servings of cake, Mama reached on top of the refrigerator and grabbed the carton of eggs.

"Here, Sofia! This is your birthday present from all of us!"

"Eh . . . thank you," I said as I took the carton. Everybody started laughing.

"Open it, *Comadre* Sofia!" Lucy said, kneeling on her chair.

Papa and Mama were standing next to me, their arms around each other.

Inside I found twelve *cascarones*.

"Well, thank you," I said, smiling.

"Sofia," Lucy pointed. "Look at those four. Those are your presents. Open them!"

I took the one at the corner. It was bright yellow with a drawing of two people at a sewing machine. I turned the egg and found a drawing of five stick people in a car. "That's from me!" said Berta, smiling.

"Do you want me to crack it on your head?" I asked, remembering the mustard-filled *cascarone* she had smashed on my head many Easters before.

"No!" They were all laughing. "Break it over your cake plate, but carefully."

I took the egg, cracked it around the top, hitting it on the edge of the plate. I pulled off the shell pieces.

A small plastic box on a key chain fell into the plate. I picked it up. "Look inside! But point it at the light!" Berta said. I took the box and peered through the small hole at the end, pointing the other end at the lightbulb. I started to laugh. It was the picture of Mama and me dancing at Berta's *quinceañera*.

"It's like you and your mama dancing on the big

drive-in screen!" said Berta. "And do you know what the two drawings on the *cascarone* are?" I smiled and shook my head. "One is of you and me at the sewing machine, making your school dresses. The other . . . well . . . I finally got your papa and mama to agree to use my car to take you up to Austin. And I'm going too!"

I gave her a big hug.

"Now open Mama's! It's the red one!" Lucy said.

I took the red *cascarone* and studied the drawings. One was of my shirt with the holy host inside the pocket. The other was of Berta and me biting and kicking each other over a candy bar. I cracked the egg, peeled it open, and pulled out a greenish rosary.

"It glows in the dark!" Mama said. "And I made it myself! Thank God and the Virgin that I finally found the keys to my chest, for I was secretly hiding it there. It's for your home altar at school. And I thought you'd like a glow-in-the-dark one since I remembered how you and your papa went through all that mess and trouble catching all those poor fireflies and smearing them all over your faces and arms, just to glow in the dark."

"Mama, thanks." I glanced at Berta, who was biting her lip to keep from cracking up.

"Papa's is next!" Lucy gave me the blue one with the silver stars and the yellow paper crown. It had two drawings: one of Papa and me cleaning beans, the other of Lucy and me coloring eggs on the porch.

A small wooden figure fell out. "Do you know who

she is?" Papa said, smiling. "I finally finished carving her this morning." I looked more closely.

"Is it a saint?" I turned it around.

"It's not just any saint, *mi'ja*. It's *your* saint, Saint Sofia. Remember we named you after Saint Sofia since you chose to be born on her feast day—August first."

"Thank you, Papa."

"But, *mi'ja*, I want you to always remember, and especially when you're far away at school, that Saint Sofia represents the gift of divine wisdom. Take her with you so that you can marry divine wisdom with everything you do."

"Now mine!" said Lucy, jumping up and down and handing me the green *cascarone*.

"Now, *Comadre* Lucy," I said. "It's not a real egg this time, is it?"

"No!" she said, beaming.

"Is that the three *comadres* in Berta's car?" I pointed to the black crayon drawing on the egg.

"Yes! And I'm the one driving!" she whispered. I cracked it open and out fell eight quarters.

"It's to buy candy at that school!" Lucy said. I hugged her hard, knowing it was all the money she had saved up in her pink Barbie bank. I started to cry.

Then Papa touched my shoulder and handed me his guitar. He whispered. I took the guitar and started to play "Julia," the *vals* he had just finished teaching me. Papa took Mama in his arms and waltzed her around the kitchen. Berta grabbed Lucy and they stumbled around, making it up as they went along. I played my heart out.

After the *vals*, Lucy raced up and smashed a *cascarone* on my head. Confetti flew everywhere as we ran around breaking the rest of the *cascarones* on each other's heads.

Later, after Berta had gone home and Mama and Lucy were praying the rosary in the other room, Papa came into the kitchen, where I was strumming the guitar. I looked at him and thought, was it the crazy *canicula* that was making me wonder whether I should actually go away . . . now that everyone seemed so happy for me?

"*Mi'ja*, this is for you too," Papa said, handing me a *cascarone* painted to look like the globe of the world, with the sun, moon, and stars on the paper top. "It's *my* secret *cascarone*. But don't open it now. Wait until later."

I held it carefully. "But when can I open it, Papa?"

"Oh, you'll know," he said, smiling. "And that little Saint Sofia will always be around to help you too. Good night, *mi'ja*." He kissed me.

I put the *cascarone* in my shirt pocket along with Saint Sofia. I now felt that I would never be alone, even far away from home, and that I could finally start packing.

My birthday wish had come true.

Another Mundo

We woke up super early one Sunday late in August, packed my things into Berta's car, and set out for Austin.

I had spent the previous day saying my good-byes to all my relatives and finishing my packing. I must've been hugged, kissed, prayed over, and drenched with holy water a thousand times.

Mama insisted on my taking the family's one suitcase, which was hard plastic, avocado green. It needed a rope to stay closed. There I put the five new dresses, other clothes, and the copy of *Don Quixote* Papa had given me, saying, "It'll inspire and amuse you, *mi'ja*, on this new quest of yours."

Then Mama presented me with a sealed cardboard box. "This is for your room altar." I looked at Berta and rolled my eyes. Mama returned with a second box. "The first box was for your soul; this one is for your body," she said, putting it beside the other one.

"What's inside, Mama?" I said as I emptied the top drawer of the bureau I shared with Lucy. She could start using it now.

"A big bag of empanadas and a brand-new box of Ibarra Mexican chocolate."

After Mama left the room, Berta started laughing. "I can just picture you using your *comadre* props—the *pan dulce* and hot chocolate—to try making friends with those snooty girls. I don't think they've ever seen a homemade empanada before, or talked to a Mexican American, for that matter."

I shook my head and went on emptying the drawer, trying to find little treasures to give Lucy. She happily took my rose quartz, my mariachi puppet, a clown pin, some miniature Mexican ceramic pots, and an old set of tiny worry dolls. And she was especially excited when I gave her my tequila worm piggy bank with a whole dollar inside.

But she refused my three-inch praying mantis floating in a bottle of alcohol, my slingshot, my bag of marbles, my wooden top, my plastic magnifying glass that I used to fry ants, and my fishing knife. I knew Berta wouldn't want any of these treasures either, so I put them in a shoe box. "No wonder you're always wearing the same jeans and shirt," Berta said. "Your drawer is completely full of *junk*!" I just smiled.

As Papa drove, he drank black coffee from a thermos, while the rest of us ate our breakfast egg tacos, which Mama had made early that morning.

"Have you heard anything about your roommate?" Berta bit into her chocolate-topped *concha*.

"All I know is that her name is Brooke, Brooke Fisher. And that my dorm is called Ames Hall."

About halfway there, we stopped in Three Rivers to eat lunch at a little Mexican restaurant right off the highway.

"Sofia," Mama said, "order a big platter of cheese en-chiladas, for it'll be a while before you can come back home. And for all we know, until then you'll be eating, what—celery sticks and crackers?"

After I forced the last forkful of enchiladas down, Mama insisted on ordering a plate of hot *sopapillas*, which we dipped in honey.

Then off we went again, this time with the three *comadres* in front and Berta driving. Papa fell asleep, while Mama opened her big purse, took out her rosary, and started praying silently. Mama's *santos* were taped onto Berta's dashboard. Lucy's *comadre* job was to keep finding a clear Top 40 radio station as we drove, passing tiny towns and ranches, but mostly mesquite trees, tumble-weeds, and bushes.

In Austin, Papa drove around and around until he found a little motel called Casa Mexico. He rented one room with two queen-size beds. We went across the street to a Mexican café before turning in for the night.

The next morning, we started toward Saint Luke's. I hadn't been able to eat any of the huevos rancheros at breakfast.

"Sofia," Mama said, "are you feeling okay?"

"Yes!" I said, trying to sound cheerful.

"You look as gray as when you put that holy host in your pocket." Berta and Lucy started laughing. I forced myself to laugh too. I didn't mention that I had put Saint Sofia in my shirt pocket that morning.

Papa turned at a granite marker with the words SAINT LUKE'S EPISCOPAL SCHOOL etched in big block letters and proceeded up a winding hill behind a brand-new silver Mercedes. I felt a headache coming on. I turned around and felt a little better when I saw an old white Volvo station wagon with a couple of dents behind us.

After three miles of winding up the hill, we passed through a stone gate.

"Wow!" said Lucy. "It's like a magic kingdom."

And it did look like a small magic town on top of an enchanted hill, with the spacious green playing fields, a chapel steeple at the very top and center, and the grand stone buildings around a large quadrangle. There were numerous gardens and small courtyards. As we drove around trying to find Ames Hall, we passed an observatory, riding stables, gyms, tennis courts, a swimming pool, faculty homes, a golf course, and the dining hall.

THe TeQuiLa WORM

"So where's Wal-Mart?" said Berta.

"Yes, and what about the drive-in, the *panaderia,* the *raspa* stand? *Dios mio!* I wouldn't need the *canicula* to go crazy here," said Mama, shaking her head.

"Yeah!" said Lucy. Papa caught my eye in the rearview mirror and just smiled.

Ames Hall was a two-story white stone building with a small garden in front. A golden retriever was fast asleep on the trimmed grass.

"Look, Sofia!" Lucy said. "Why don't you get a pet too!"

Papa parked between the same silver Mercedes and white Volvo I'd seen on the road.

"Your dorm reminds me of my army barracks," Papa said as we climbed the stairs and walked down the hall to my room. The place *was* spartan, with rooms opening onto a long stone hallway. There was a bathroom at each end, and a faculty family lived in one corner of the building. There was also a common room on the first floor, which had a fireplace and a bookcase. The walls were covered with framed pictures of students at sports, at teas, at graduation.

"Where's the TV?" asked Lucy, looking around.

"And the kitchen?" said Mama as we kept looking for my room and smiling politely at the other girls and families walking around carrying lamps, suitcases, plants, rugs.

"I don't think there is a TV *or* a kitchen," I said.

"*Dios mio!* No Wal-Mart, no *panaderia,* no *raspa* stand, no drive-in, no H.E.B., no TV, and now *no kitchen?*

Are you sure this isn't a reform school, Sofia?" Mama said, shaking her head.

"Here it is," I said, pointing to my name.

"They're like cantina doors," said Berta as we walked through two swinging doors. The room was empty except for a box on one of the two beds.

"Wow!" said Lucy. "And I thought you were going to live like a princess. This is no bigger than our room at home." The room was about twelve feet by fifteen. On each side there were one metal frame bed, a desk, a chair, a bookcase, a three-drawer bureau, and an open closet. The only really nice part was that it had two windows overlooking the garden outside.

The cantina doors flew open and in walked a tall blond girl wearing green slacks, a monogrammed pink shirt, and brown loafers.

"Have you seen Brooke?"

Silence.

"No," I said.

"Oh, you must be Sofia?"

"Yes. Hi."

"I'm Terry Gibbs, and my room is just across the hall. Listen, I know Brooke from before. We go to the same country club. Would you mind terribly if we switched?"

"Switched?"

"Yes, I would really like to room with Brooke. We could just switch rooms now and it would be no trouble since neither of us has unpacked."

"Well, I don't even know if we can, if it's allowed, you know. And anyway, I'd like to think about it first."

"Okay, but let me know as soon as possible."

"Okay."

Terry turned and left.

"These people have no manners," Mama said, shaking her head.

"Sofia," Lucy said, "come back home with us." Papa just looked at me.

I made myself laugh. "Let's hurry with my things, since you still have the long drive back." When we went back to Berta's car, I saw Terry taking a large stereo set from the trunk of the silver Mercedes. There was a man in a black vest and slacks helping her, saying, "Yes, Miss Terry. Yes, Miss Terry."

Then Terry started running up the hill. "Brooke! Brooke!" she said.

A girl with shiny brown hair and bright green eyes was walking down the hill with her parents. As they got closer, I saw she was wearing old sneakers, faded jeans, and a white shirt with a tiny green alligator.

Terry air-kissed the girl and shook hands with her parents. I was taking the box with the altar stuff out of the trunk when I felt a tap on my shoulder.

"Hey, Sofia, this is Brooke," Terry said. "So do you want to switch?"

"Ah . . . hi, Brooke," I said, shaking her hand.

"Terry," Brooke said, "I want to room with Sofia." She smiled at me.

"Oh! Okay." Terry's face turned red. "But promise you'll let me know if you change your mind. And how's your brother Chris? I'm *sure* he'll get into Harvard."

Brooke just nodded. She introduced her parents to me and met my family.

We spent the next two hours unpacking.

"Now let me set up your room altar," Mama said as she set the box on top of my freshly made bed. Brooke had already hung a framed, signed Chagall print on her wall—one with a lady's face that could be seen as two different faces. She'd put a small Persian rug by her bed and placed a cut-glass vase with pink and yellow roses on her bookcase. Her bedspread was a quilt with a pretty repeating fan pattern.

"Mama," I said, shaking my head as she tore the tape off the box and pulled out a yellow votive candle, a ten-inch statue of the Virgin of Guadalupe with lightbulb and cord, the glow-in-the-dark rosary, a framed print of the Guardian Angel, and my late grandmother's favorite saint, the black San Martín de Porres. It was so old and badly chipped that his face was chalk white and his body rotated in three broken parts on a thin wire. Last was a twelve-inch bleeding Christ on a wooden cross. Berta kept biting her lip to keep from laughing. Papa was sitting on one corner of the bed, calm and smiling, wearing his brown and white boots. "Now, where should I put your altar?" said Mama.

"Put it on top of her bookcase," Lucy said, "so everyone can see it!" Then Brooke walked in carrying a white orchid, which she placed next to the vase of roses on top of her bookcase.

"Cool!" Brooke said, smiling. "Is that for your home altar?"

"Yes, but how do you know?" I said.

"My parents run a foundation for schools in Latin America. So I've seen pictures of them."

"See, *mi'ja*," Mama said as she proceeded to arrange my room altar on top of my bookcase. "And it's for you, too, Brooke," Mama said, turning and smiling at her. "It'll sanctify your room." She took her plastic bottle of holy water from her purse and started sprinkling.

After all the students and their families gathered in the courtyard in front of the chapel for a welcome tea with the headmaster, it was time for Berta and my family to head back home.

"Those sandwiches were so tiny," Mama said as we walked toward Berta's car, "like for a doll. And where was the coffee? The hot chocolate? *Ay, mi'ja,* I'm so worried for you: your dorm looks like a prison, and the food . . . It's like stepping into another *mundo*. And here I thought that it was the *canicula* that made things crazy. Listen, when you get back to your room, break open the other box and have yourself an empanada or two. And be sure to share them with Brooke. She's too skinny and pale."

The three *comadres* and Papa started laughing. He put his arm around Mama and gave her a kiss on her rouged cheek, which matched her pretty red dress.

"Take a big bite, Sofia!" Berta said, unwrapping a Hershey's chocolate bar.

"Only if you put your fingers at the tip!" I said, and bit down. Mama and Papa walked on ahead of us, arm in arm.

"And, Sofia," Berta said, "here's my advice to you: one, comb that crazy hair of yours; two, always, *always* button your buttons *straight*; and three, kick that girl Terry out of your mind.

"Oh, and also remember our promise to Tía Petra about getting good at becoming faraway *comadres*."

"With me, too!" said Lucy.

"Yes, Lucy, of course, you too!" I said, touching her head. "And remember to write me about your *quinceañera*."

"*Quinceañera? Whose* quinceañera?" said Mama, turning around.

"Mine, Mama! I'm starting to plan it!" said Lucy, beaming.

Papa laughed. Mama shook her head. "*Ay, mi'ja*, now, *that's* a record. You need to tell Clara so . . ." Mama stopped. "Sofia, what story do you want Clara to tell as she goes around with her story bag? And don't say *none*." Even with her stroke, Clara was still telling her stories, though now the stories were written on paper and attached to the things in her bag, and we all took turns reading them for her.

"That my dream came true, Mama . . . thanks to you all."

"Okay. Now come here," she said as she pulled a pair of scissors from her big purse. "And stand still." Before I knew it, Mama had cut off a three-inch lock of my hair.

"*Mama!* What are you doing?"

"Now give me one of your socks."

"*What?*" Students and parents were passing by.

"*Hurry!*" Berta and Lucy pulled off my sneaker, then my sock, tossing it to Mama.

"Good! I'm going to make a Sofia doll from this sock. I'll attach your hair to it and give it to Clara for when she tells your story." They all laughed.

I kissed everyone good-bye. When I heard Papa's door slam, I felt very much alone. I stood there waving until the car disappeared. Then, with my heart and head pounding, I slowly went up the stairs to my room. Was this the right time to open Papa's secret *cascarone*?

I stopped and reached into my shirt pocket and pulled out the little wooden carving of Saint Sofia. I suddenly remembered Papa's words of many years before, that our side of town had its own wealth and warmth. I finally understood what he'd meant.

I started climbing the stairs again, with Saint Sofia back in my shirt pocket, wondering if this strange world would somehow help me understand better not only the other side but my side as well.

Saints at Saint Luke's

TERRY was on Brooke's bed, crying, and Brooke was saying, "Everything will be okay." I started to leave, but Brooke caught my arm and mouthed *stay*.

I went to my desk, took out Tía Petra's plastic-covered notebook, and started writing my first letter home. After about ten minutes, Terry left, still weepy.

"She's something," Brooke said, sitting on her bed with her back against the wall.

"What do you mean?"

"Well, she's already obsessed about getting into one of the big three."

"The big three?"

"Yes, you know, Harvard, Yale, or Princeton."

"Oh . . . is Terry a scholar?"

"No!" Brooke said, laughing. "She's average, at best. Now, don't get me wrong. She's not dumb, either. But she's, well, a headmaster's choice."

"A what?"

"She got in because her parents make a lot of money."

"Oh." I blinked. "But why is she so obsessed about getting into the big three?"

"Because she wants what she thinks comes with it."

"What's that?"

"Privilege. Money. Power. Her wedding in the *New York Times* social pages. All that."

"But . . . why was she crying?"

"Well . . . Terry got dumped here. See, her parents are going through this messy divorce. And she wants to room with me because she likes my brother, Tiff, who's graduating this year."

"I thought his name was Chris?"

Brooke started laughing. "His name is Christopher, but we've always called him Tiff. I don't know where Terry got *Chris*. Go figure."

"I see," I said, thinking that there was a whole lot more I *didn't* see. And I had thought getting the five new dresses was going to be the hard part.

The cantina doors flew open. It was Terry. "Hey, Sofia, I hear you're here on a scholarship. Is that right?"

"Yes."

"And there're three other Mexican Americans on scholarship too?"

"Yes."

"So where are *they*?"

"In the boys' dorm."

"Oh," Terry said as she walked over to my bookcase and picked up the wooden crucifix with the bleeding Christ. "You're also Catholic, right?"

"Yes." My head was starting to hurt.

"Don't you think Mexicans are obsessed with death?"

"Terry!" said Brooke, taking the crucifix and putting it back. "And aren't parvenus obsessed with money and status and marrying old money?" Terry turned red and stormed out.

"What's a parvenu?" I said.

"New money. What Terry is all about."

"Oh." I was more confused than ever, and school hadn't even officially started yet.

The next morning, I woke to the sound of a loud, clanging bell. I thought about the student who'd been assigned the job of ringing the school bell for the entire week—for each wake-up; for each class; for chapel; for mail call; for breakfast, lunch, and dinner; and even for milk and cookies after evening study hall. We all had jobs.

Mine were to clean room twenty-four every morning and to put out the student mail.

Living by bells turned out to be only the first of a long string of surprises.

There was the *total* lack of privacy. I realized this as I was dressing for my first dinner. Brooke seemed used to it, quickly slipping into a tan cotton dress with brass buttons, and white pumps.

I stood there in my jeans. I didn't mind being naked in my room at home with Lucy. But I didn't even know Brooke. Could I go change in one of the bathroom stalls? No! Why was I so modest? Because I was Catholic? Because I was Mexican? Both?

The bell for dinner started clanging.

"Sofia, aren't you coming to dinner?" Brooke said.

"Eh . . . yes. I was just . . . wondering what dress to wear."

She looked into my closet. "How about this one? It's *gorgeous*." *What? The bedsheet?*

"Okay," I said, laughing. I changed in a wink.

While walking to the dining room, Brooke said, "That's such a pretty dress, really. Think I can borrow it?"

"Oh, sure." I couldn't wait to tell Berta.

A seating chart was posted outside. I was at table nine.

The long table stood by a window overlooking the Colorado River. There were four chairs on each side and one at each end.

I stood by a chair as others did. Then Marcos walked over.

"Sofia! Are you at table nine too?"

"Yes!" I said, smiling. I hadn't seen him since suffering through those tests in Harlingen. Marcos looked like Felix the Cat in his dark coat and tie. He already resembled a cat in his quick and light-footed ways.

"Terrific! Is Mr. Smith your faculty advisor too? This is his table, you know."

"Yes."

A chime sounded. Students and faculty hurried to their seats. Mr. Smith took his spot at the head. He was tall, with curly black hair. His wife took the chair at the other end. She was wearing a suit and an elegant silk scarf. Our table had four boys and four girls, and Marcos stood next to me.

The headmaster said a prayer. Then everyone took their seats. The table was set with linen, silver, and china. The food was brought over on a big silver platter. *Steak!* And *everyone* got one. I had never eaten a whole steak before. I remembered Papa's saying, "Sofia, beans are better than any steak." I missed Papa's beans, but the steak was really good too!

"Sofia, how was your summer?" Mr. Smith said.

Silence.

"Excuse me, Sofia. I was asking about your summer. Charles here spent it biking in France." Charles was blond and tanned, and he was staring.

"Eh . . . fine. It was fine, Mr. Smith, thanks." Imagine telling them about the cucumber shed!

Mr. Smith smiled.

After supper, Marcos walked me to my dorm. I started laughing.

"What's so funny?"

"Well, when Mr. Smith asked about my summer, I was about to say that I'd spent it sorting cucumbers at a packing shed."

"Why didn't you?"

"They would have choked on their steak, especially that Charles guy." Marcos laughed.

"How's your dorm?"

"Like a monk's cell. They should at least let us have a refrigerator. I'm going to starve before school even starts."

"I have a big bag of empanadas and a box of Mexican chocolate. Want some?"

"Ibarra's Mexican chocolate? Sweet or semisweet?"

"Semisweet."

"You said the magic words! I *love* that stuff."

"But how are you going to make it? Hot plates aren't allowed."

"Make it? I eat it by the disk. I used to eat three a day."

I ran upstairs and brought Marcos three disks.

"Thank you, thank you! You don't know how happy you've made me." He unwrapped one and took a huge bite. "Wow! This stuff makes me feel like I'm back in McAllen."

I laughed. "Have you met the other valley students?"

"Yeah, they're in my dorm. One is Paco, from Brownsville. And Carlos, from Edinburg. But that dorm is something else."

"What do you mean?"

"Well, the senior guys rule. Last night this new ninth grader mouthed off to a senior guy. The next minute he was outside naked, begging to be let in. The senior guys finally let him, but only after he apologized. How are things in *your* dorm?"

"Okay, so far."

Then the bell for study hall started clanging. Marcos ran to get his books, waving.

My English class was in a room with a big round table with eleven chairs. Brooke sat next to me. She said, "Mr. Maxwell is brilliant, but tough, really tough."

The door flew open and in stumbled a stooped man smoking a pipe and wearing a squashed hat and a rumpled tweed jacket, with a chocolate cocker spaniel at his side.

"Eh . . . good morning, class! This is my dog, Hemingway. He . . . he *loves,* yes, really loves books . . . novels, especially . . . and writing, reading . . . well, you can . . . learn a lot . . . from Hemingway . . . my dog . . . but . . . he's on sabbatical, you know . . . so he'll just be sleeping . . . yes, sleeping there in the . . . corner. . . .

"Yes, yes. *The Great Gatsby*. F. Scott Fitzgerald." Mr. Maxwell looked at his wrist, searched his pockets, opened his jacket, took off his hat. "Eh . . . lost my watch . . . again. No matter. Class! Listen up! You have *exactly* forty-five minutes to write an essay on the significance of the green light in *The Great Gatsby*. Now, *go!*"

We froze. I must've turned as white as a ghost. Then, in a split second, notebooks snapped, papers flew, pens popped, and the class tore into writing. My heart pounded, my adrenaline pumped as I wrote. I felt terrified and electrified at the same time.

"*Stop!*" Mr. Maxwell said. The bell started clanging. He reached into his jacket pocket and pulled out a dog biscuit shaped like a bone. Hemingway started chomping.

"I'll grade these tonight. Get them back to you tomorrow. Tomorrow's assignment is to read *To the Lighthouse*. Virginia Woolf." He took the papers, rolled them up, stuffed them into his jacket pocket, and slammed his shoulder into the doorframe on the way out.

Sports were another surprise. It was field hockey term. Monday through Friday, from three to five in the afternoon, we whacked each other's shins, knees, and worse with those blasted hockey sticks. I was black and blue all over.

Brooke and I were getting along well off the field, but there were times when I wanted to slam her with my hockey stick and kick her even harder. She was good, but too often she ran with the ball when she ought to have passed. We lost our first game because of her.

At practice the next day, Brooke did the exact same thing. As we were dressing for dinner, I said, "Brooke, why don't you ever pass the ball?"

"Sofia, your problem is that you *always* pass the ball. How do you plan to ever score, to stand out?"

That night, Brooke slept soundly, while I stared at the glow-in-the-dark rosary. I thought about how much I missed my family. Papa, Berta, even Lucy would've passed the ball. That was how teams worked, that was what I'd been taught. I glanced at Brooke. She was nice and all, but we'd never get as close as I was with Berta.

Chapel was different too. When I entered for my first weekday service, I found not only no Virgin of Guadalupe there, but no saints, either—not even Saint Luke. There was only a thin wooden cross hanging suspended at the front. *So this is the main difference between being Episcopalian and Catholic,* I thought.

Imagine my shock when I walked into chapel for Sunday service and found my Virgin of Guadalupe all lit up at the very front of the chapel. When the Episcopal priest walked up to begin the service, he immediately unplugged her and hid her behind a big plant on the floor.

An hour later I was summoned to see my advisor, Mr. Smith. "Sofia," he said, smiling, "is this yours?"

I wanted to die. He flipped the plastic Virgin over and pointed to my name in big black letters on the bottom. I mumbled, "Yes, sir, she's mine, but I have no idea how she got into the chapel."

Mr. Smith smiled again and handed her back to me. "Sofia, try keeping her in your room."

A week later the chipped saint made his way into the chapel. He was soon returned to me, as were eventually the votive candle, the glow-in-the-dark rosary, and the Guardian Angel, who took turns appearing at Sunday services. This was even after I'd put them all back in the box and then hidden them inside my suitcase.

I missed my room altar, especially at night, when I thought of home most. I liked looking at the glow-in-the-dark rosary and remembering my last birthday. I especially missed Lucy and hearing her giggle at the crazy stories I told her before going off to sleep.

I wanted to kick whoever was taking my saints. This was worse than when our dorm woke to find every single one of our bras missing. We later found them all hooked together and festooned across a classroom—with mine being the only ones bearing my name in bold black letters—something Mama had insisted upon.

One afternoon I went into my room and found Brooke and Terry arguing. Terry was bright red and

Brooke was holding a piece of paper. A bottle of tequila stood on my bookcase, where my room altar used to be. I froze. *I could get kicked out for having liquor in my room!*

"Come on, Terry, apologize to Sofia, or I'll tell her and everybody else, including Tiff," said Brooke, staring at Terry.

"Tell me what?" I said. Terry kept her eyes fixed on the stone floor. She was turning redder and redder.

"Okay! Here, Sofia," Brooke said, handing me the paper. Terry stormed out.

I took the piece of paper and read it, then reread it: *Everything from Mexico—including tequila—has worms. So why don't you and your morbid saints wiggle back across the border?*

Brooke said, "I'm really sorry, Sofia! It was Terry's idea of a cool prank, one she thought would make her popular. But it was just as dumb as she is. Don't take it personally. She is just mean, mean, mean."

I walked over and picked up the tequila bottle. I shook the bottle and stared as the white worm slowly settled back to the bottom. So it had been Terry all along. The one who'd plugged in my Virgin at Sunday chapel and later made all my other *santos* appear as well. Rooting around in my things! And now this, this note. I started to laugh, remembering Taco Head. *Time to kick Terry's butt.*

I took a deep breath, crumpled up the stupid note, and then kicked it across the hall to Terry's room. She was sitting on her bed, paging through a teen magazine. "Hey,

Terry, my family didn't cross the border; it crossed us. We've been here for over three hundred years, before the U.S. drew those lines. And here's a little secret: only a bottle of mescal has a *real* worm inside." I dropped the bottle next to her on the bed. I went back to my room and took down my suitcase, and Brooke and I put all my *santos* back on my bookcase.

News of Terry's mean prank was all over campus the next morning. She found her mailbox jammed with hate mail and had to report to the headmaster.

I found a card from Marcos in my mailbox: *Sofia, you kicked that girl good! And for all of us! How about kicking the soccer ball with me on Saturday? And please, please bring a disk of your Ibarra chocolate. We can share it and dream about being back in McAllen.* I smiled.

As mail monitor, I just kept kicking hate mail into Terry's box, enjoying it more and more.

The Panty-Hose Baby

"**IT'S** like being in a pressure cooker," I said to Brooke as we raced back to the dorm after field hockey practice to shower and dress for dinner. "I mean, I hardly find time, or the energy, to even think of my family." And there were still hours of study hall before lights out. Then the same every-minute-filled cycle started too early the next morning with the clang, clang, clanging of the wake-up bell.

"So it's working," Brooke said, tossing her hockey stick in the air and catching it.

"What's working?"

"These sunup-to-sundown-filled days. Take Tiff. It's gotten to the point where the back-and-forth from here to home makes him feel awkward at *home*. It's as though his school friends are his new family."

I thought about what Brooke said as I stood brushing my teeth before lights-out in front of a row of sinks. As I walked down the hallway to my room, I heard the stereos: Rock music blared from one room; classical from another; then, jazz . . . It was as though every girl was trying to assert whatever individuality she had left in the few desperate minutes before lights-out, before we were all thrown together into sleeping, eating, studying, playing, praying, and doing everything together again the next day.

As I lay in bed staring at the glow-in-the-dark rosary, the *vals* "Julia" started playing in my mind, and I saw Papa waltzing with Mama around the kitchen table and Berta and Lucy stumbling, making up the waltz as they went along. Did the girls in the dorm play their music to conjure up some image of home, of their past?

I thought about how Tiff felt awkward at home and how he felt that his school friends were now his new family. From all Brooke had said, her family was warm and close. And they lived right here in Austin.

I leaped out of bed and took Tía Petra's plastic-covered notebook from my desk drawer. I grabbed a pen and my secret flashlight. Brooke was fast asleep. I got back into bed, pulled the sheet over my head, and clicked the flashlight on. I started writing. It started as a letter to Papa, but it turned into a story about the image of my family all waltzing around the kitchen table. I made my characters talk: Berta said, "Stop stepping on my toes, Lucy, or I'll bite you!" "Okay, Berta, but only if you pop out of my *quinceañera* cake!" This made me laugh.

I finished my story at two in the morning, with Papa kissing me goodnight. I smiled, turned off the flashlight, and went happily to sleep. I felt they were all in the room with me.

I woke early the next morning and reread my story. I called it "Waltzing to 'Julia,' Around the Kitchen Table, in McAllen." I started writing a letter home. Now, more than ever, I didn't want to lose touch with my family. I smiled. How could I? I kept getting more and more wacky packages from Mama.

The very first week at Saint Luke's, Mama sent me a round brown rock the size of a fist with a picture of Yoda on it.

Mama called. "Sofia, did you get my package?"

"Yes, thanks. Is it . . . a rock?"

"It's a paperweight, Sofia, for your desk. But Lucy is making hers a pet."

"A *pet*?"

"Yes, a pet rock. I put a rose on hers, a picture I cut from a *True Confessions* magazine."

"Where did you get the picture of Yoda?"

"Yoda? Who's Yoda?"

"The picture on mine."

"Oh, I didn't know that funny-looking elf had a name. He's perfect since he has pointy ears like yours."

Perfect—as perfect as the "panty-hose baby" she'd made for me years ago from old pairs of hose and dressed in overalls, a baseball cap, and tiny red sneakers.

She insisted on taking him to H.E.B., the grocery store, and putting him in the shopping-cart seat. We went up one aisle and down another, with Mama talking to "her baby," Jesus. I followed her to the candy section, where she started showing bag after jumbo bag of candy to Jesus, asking whether he wanted lollipops or candy bars or bubble gum.

She kept doing this until she finally got a couple of stares. The cart was now stacked full with bags of potato chips, cream-filled donuts, and a big tub of lard.

After making sure the stares were still on her, Mama headed to the beer department.

As she was picking up a six-pack of Tecate and another of Corona, she got a tap on her shoulder. Mama turned, a pack in each hand, to find a tall woman with red lipstick and a man with a black pin saying MANAGER.

They glared at Mama. The man said, "It is *not* allowed to leave a baby unattended."

Mama grabbed Jesus and tossed him high into the air. They gasped.

She caught him and yanked off his cap. They gasped louder! Jesus didn't have a face.

Mama laughed loudly, wiggling Jesus, and said, "Don't worry! He's just a panty-hose baby!"

That would make a good story too, I thought as I kept writing my letter home.

Aside from the Yoda rock, I received a tiny pair of pants she'd made out of two dishtowels. They were for the kitchen, she said over the phone, for storing the plastic bags from the supermarket. Now, instead of stuffing them into a drawer or behind the stove, I could stuff them into the pair of pants. And once it got full, it looked great because the stomach expanded and looked like the pants had just swallowed a big watermelon. You hung the pants on a hook and stuffed the plastic bags through the waist on top. Then you retrieved them as needed by simply pulling the plastic bags out of the legs below.

"Thank you, Mama," I said over the phone. "But remember, there's no kitchen here."

"So use it for your socks. But be sure to hang it on a hook, so everyone can see it. Lucy just loves hers. I'm making one for Berta!"

Then there were the delicate flowers and birds she carefully crocheted on covers for rolls of toilet paper. Lucy

THE TEQUILA WORM

got a green one; I got purple; Berta got red. The strange dusting gloves she made by attaching hundreds and hundreds of strands of yarn to a perfectly good glove. I felt a jolt when I opened the package and found what looked like a giant spider inside. Mine had taken the longest to make, she said when she called. She used ten different colors of yarn, whereas Lucy's was all just a shocking pink, the glove as well as the yarn. She was making one for Berta, too.

"Isn't it great?" she said. "Go and try it out."

I slowly slipped the glove on and then moved my fingers. It was the strangest thing, with hundreds of stands of yarn of all colors—dangling from all five fingers and the whole palm.

"Go dust your bookcase—your room altar!"

I walked over to the bookcase in the corner and slowly started rubbing the plastic Virgin and the chipped saint. I couldn't even feel the surfaces I was dusting. It felt like my hand was floating.

"Now, isn't that great!" she said. "And you can't even see the dirt on the glove. And I bet it'll be a big hit with your friends, and soon you'll be calling me to make them some too. And that's okay. But don't lend yours out, except to Brooke, or you'll never see it again."

I eventually received the embroidered tortilla holder she made by sewing two handkerchiefs together. The yarn cap with dangling plastic circles that looked like shark gills. The basket made from the plastic rings that hold six-packs of pop cans together. Styrofoam clown heads for the tops of *all* my pens *and* pencils. "Aren't they great! You can talk to them as you write!" And countless other things—just for me.

But one thing I sent back was something she'd made by trapping my old Barbie doll in a huge ruffled red dress, crocheted and decorated with yards and yards of shiny bows and lace. I just couldn't believe it. Barbie seemed to weigh a ton.

"What's at the bottom?" I asked on the phone, for all that showed of my former doll were her little head, neck, and arms.

"Rocks."

"Rocks?"

"Yes, rocks. She's a doorstop. I said to myself, what can I do with her to make her useful again? So that's when I got the idea."

"But she's a doll, Mama."

"Not anymore. And anyway, her left leg kept falling off. Remember?"

"But what do you want me to do with her? You know that my dorm room has swinging doors about two feet off the floor."

She finally agreed to let me send her back—until I got a *real* door. She said, "I wish you were more like Lucy. *She* always loves my gifts."

I said, "Lucy might love the Barbie doorstop."

"Lucy's already taken care of. I'm making her a doorstop too, using her old Easter bunny."

"You're putting a dress on her pink rabbit?"

"Sure! It'll look great!"

As I was addressing the envelope, the wake-up bell started clanging. Brooke yawned, stumbling out of bed.

"I had a dream about you last night, Sofia. You and your father were waltzing around this kitchen table. I think you've told me so many stories about your family, especially about your father, that I've now started even dreaming about them." *Wow! My secret story did bring them here!*

I called home that evening. Lucy answered, laughing.

"What's so funny?"

"You!"

"Why?"

"Mama just finished making the Sofia doll for Clara. And it's *so* funny-looking! Looks just like you!"

"Gee, thanks."

"No, you should see it, Sofia. I mean, it's so funny how she attached your crazy hair to the sock doll she made." I could hear Berta laughing in the back. "She even put pointy ears, using buttons."

"Send it, Lucy. I want to see it." *So I can destroy it! Imagine Clara going around with this crazy Sofia doll!*

"No way! It's going straight to Clara first thing tomorrow morning. You'd kick it to threads if you saw it."

"Well, it sure sounds like the *canicula* lives there at home—and for the entire three hundred sixty-five days a year!"

"We miss you, Sofia. How are things up there?"

"Okay. A little crazy. But most of the students are nice, or, at least, nice enough. Now let me say hi to Berta. . . ."

"I've gotten three more requests to borrow the bed-sheet dress, Berta. You're amazing! And thanks for sending me those chocolate bars. How are you?"

"Well, Jamie and I are still together."

"I *know*. You've sent fifty pictures of Jamie so far." We laughed. "But how's Lucy?"

"Boy, she misses you. She's always talking about you. How's Brooke? Marcos? Classes?"

"Brooke's fine. Nice, but still hogging the ball in hockey.

"Marcos is fine too. He's funny. We kick the soccer ball around on Saturdays and catch up on our Spanish. We complain about how it's all about getting into college here, about the individual, about competition, about this thing they call character building. But we've both made friends here.

"And as for classes, the teachers are terrific. It's amazing, Berta, how hard they work. They live and work Saint Luke's, even eating all their meals with the students. So far, I'm keeping up.

"But I miss you all *so much*. Can't wait for Thanksgiving. Now let me talk to Papa. . . ."

After Papa, I spoke to Mama, and after I hung up, I started to cry. A big part of me wanted to go home. *Now.* School felt like a strange passage to . . . I didn't even know where.

My calls home were also feeling more and more like performances, always sounding cheerful. If they only knew how many times I'd been to my secret place, the old oak tree by the river, to cry from loneliness.

Later that week I received my first package from Papa. It was the tequila worm he'd promised, in a tiny empty mescal bottle. I made it part of my room altar, setting it next to Papa's secret *cascarone*. My stories were helping me feel less homesick. Now Papa had sent the *real* cure. I'd save it, just in case.

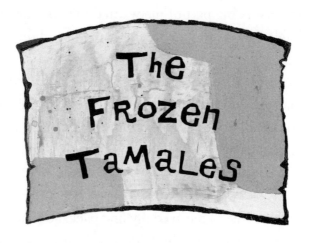

The Frozen Tamales

The school campus became a sea of Beemers and Mercedeses and one or two Fords and Volvos the Wednesday before Thanksgiving. Brooke's parents had insisted on dropping Marcos and me off at the Greyhound station in downtown Austin. This would be my first trip home, and I was *so* excited. Mama had written that Tía Petra wanted us to come over for a special surprise Thursday morning. And that the *abuelitos* were coming over for Thanksgiving dinner.

As we drove into the city, I said, "Boy, it feels exciting just to be off campus, and to see real people, stores—even traffic." We laughed.

After buying our tickets for our eight-hour trip to McAllen, Marcos and I got a cup of coffee. I said, "Are the other valley students going home too?"

"No. They're spending Thanksgiving with friends. It's too long a haul for such a short break."

"Brooke asked me to come to her house, but I *have* to go home."

"Me too."

"You know, it's strangely fun to be drinking coffee from a paper cup."

"Yes! It's another world at Saint Luke's, isn't it?" We sat down. I wondered how home would seem, now that even a bus station seemed strange. I thought of Tiff. No! I was determined to feel that home was home, that my family was my family.

Marcos said, "Don't you sometimes feel like you're at boot camp and that everything at Saint Luke's—the endless classes, sports, and such—is like one big drill to strip us and then shape us into some prep army?"

I told him what Brooke had said about Tiff.

"I believe it. Tiff's in my dorm, and I see it with some of the senior guys."

The bus to the Rio Grande Valley was announced. Marcos and I sat in the first row to look out the front window.

I said, "Is the big drill getting to you, too?"

"Sometimes. Part of me wants to just go, go, go—from Saint Luke's to college to medical school to . . . But when

I talk to Mama, I feel that I need *and* want to stay close. . . ."

"I know what you mean. I think it's different for us. I feel I'm here for my family, too, not just for myself. I love *so much* about my family, my barrio. Saint Luke's makes me appreciate them more. . . ."

"Yeah. It's confusing."

"At least the fall term exams are over."

"Wow, was that intense."

Despite the grind, I thought I was doing well in all my classes. Hockey, too. And I enjoyed hanging out with Brooke and Marcos and my other friends. But it felt good just to be sitting in a bus, looking out the window. Marcos dozed off. By the time we stopped at the tenth tiny town, I was dozing off too.

In one town we grabbed a sandwich. As we ate, Marcos said, "Hey, is Terry still being a creep?"

"The hate mail stopped her cold. And she's still getting some." Marcos laughed.

"Well, that was such a dumb thing to do. But it was funny, too, Sofia. I will never in my entire life forget the expression on your face when you saw your plastic Virgin all lit up at the front of the chapel." We both laughed.

"Oh, but that's not the half of it."

"What do you mean?"

"Well, Terry also grabbed my crucifix and said, 'Aren't Mexicans obsessed with death?'"

Marcos shook his head. "I think part of it is that death

is not even in the Saint Luke's vocabulary. I mean, there's this guy in my dorm, Skip. Well, Dan, his roommate, told me their advisor mentioned that Skip's father was terminally ill, just in case he needed help. Dan said, 'Skip, I'm so sorry about your father. Let me know if . . .' Skip said, 'My dad's fine. I don't know what you're talking about.' Two days later, he left for his father's funeral.

"But here's the weirdest part: not one single person in the dorm has mentioned a word about the death, even if they all know about it. Skip now goes around like some ghost. He's even on probation, like he can't function."

We were silent after that, until we spotted the McAllen city limits sign. Marcos and I cheered and high-fived.

And when we finally pulled into the bus station, my heart exploded with joy as I saw Papa, Mama, Lucy, and Berta waving frantically.

"Sofia! Sofia!" said Lucy, kissing me. I kissed them all. I greeted Marcos's family. Marcos and I joked about how we couldn't wait for our bus trip back. Papa was wearing his brown and white boots. He looked especially happy to see me, but I noticed a slight weariness in him.

"Papa, are you feeling all right?" I asked, putting my arm around him.

"Yes, *mi'ja*. It's so wonderful to have you home."

"Mama, Papa, can the three *comadres* drive around in Berta's car once we get home?" said Lucy. "We have a lot to catch up on."

"I told you, Sofia," said Berta. "Lucy is becoming a *comadre* at the speed of light! She's not on Mexican time like you!" I kicked Berta's shin gently.

I dropped my stuff off in our room and then discovered a dozen frozen tamales in the freezer. Wow! What a treat, especially after months of dining-hall food.

"Mama," I said, "can we have the tamales for dinner?"

"Don't even think of it, Sofia," she said. "Those are for me to eat on the Day of the Dead. And don't think you can just go over to Davila's and buy me a dozen there." She then went on and on about the tamales at Davila's, how no way was she even going to touch them, and how they should be shot for even calling them tamales, since they only put a speck or two of pork inside.

"We're having cheese enchiladas. If you want tamales, go to Davila's and buy some."

I started to laugh, for I couldn't believe anyone could feel so passionately about a dozen frozen tamales.

"Are you eating them when you go to leave flowers at the cemetery?" I asked.

"No. I'm eating them in the cemetery, but when I'm dead."

"*What?*"

Mama said, "You know I make twelve dozen tamales every year for Christmas—since you eat most of them yourself—and I make one extra dozen in case I die during the coming year. This way I can at least look forward to eating *my own tamales* on the Day of the Dead."

I remembered the hot chocolate and *pozole* Doña Virginia had made for her dead child and parents years ago, and Mama saying that they were coming to visit her on the Day of the Dead.

"I'm sorry, Mama," I said, kissing her, "I won't touch them," and I put the *tamales* back in the freezer.

Berta, Lucy, and I got into the front seat of Berta's bottle green car. It was as though I'd never left, except this time we were driving around to keep *warm*.

"Berta, pull over so I can drive!" Berta and I switched sides. I turned on the ignition and shifted to D. It felt so good to be driving.

"Lucy," I said. "How's your *quinceañera* coming along?"

"I'm still working on my boyfriend, Noe. But I now have ten *comadres,* including you and Berta. . . ."

"Wow! And I also hear you're making arts and crafts like Mama."

"Yes, but it's a secret."

"Secret? You've taken over our entire room. Lucy, where am I supposed to sleep? My bed is covered with papers, magazines, pieces of material."

"That's for my *quinceañera*. And don't forget, Sofia, you're still my maid of honor."

"Anything you say, Lucy. So, Berta, when are you and

Jamie getting married? I'll be happy to be your maid of honor for that, too."

"After graduation."

"I was *kidding*! Are you *serious*?"

"Yes, I'm serious."

"But what about college?"

"Maybe. But right now, I'm thinking of getting married, settling down."

"Settling down? Like having children?"

"Perhaps. Listen, Sofia, you're the one breaking the mold. Almost all the women in our family got married and settled down *before* finishing high school."

Silence.

"So, Sofia, are you still intent on going to college?"

"Yes."

"University of Texas in Austin?"

"Maybe I'll apply to Harvard."

"But that's many, many, many states away. You're too far already."

"So you both miss me?"

"Of course we do," said Berta.

"So you've been homesick for me, like I've been homesick for you. . . ."

"Well, surprise! I have the perfect cure!" said Berta.

She popped the glove compartment open— "Ta-dah!"—and pulled out a tiny bottle of mescal with a tequila worm inside.

"Wow!" I said. "Where did you get it?"

"That's a secret!"

We drove back to the house. "Hey, Berta, are there any glasses in your car *cantina* too?"

"Of course!" Berta popped the glove compartment and took out two shot glasses. We got out and sat on the porch.

I opened the bottle and poured. "Here, Lucy, you watch the tequila worm while your two *comadres* drink."

I sniffed the mescal. *Wow! Strong!* Berta was looking at me. "Well . . ."

"You first, Sofia. Show me how it's done."

I took a deep breath, then kicked it down. *Oh my God! Wicked! It burns! How can people drink this stuff! And why!*

"Piece of cake, Berta! Now you!" I felt mescal fumes smoking my stomach. Lucy's eyes were as big as *conchas*. Berta bit her lip. Sniffed the mescal. Squinted. Then threw it down.

"Yuck! I'm burning all the way down! Sofia, the things you make me do!"

"Berta, it was *your* idea. Remember? But now the best part. There's a tasty bite for Lucy, too." I popped the tequila worm out of the bottle. "It's only a question of who gets the head, tail, and middle. *Yummy!* Lucy, you have first pick since you didn't get to drink."

Silence.

"*Lucy?*"

"Sofia, don't be mean," Berta said. "You go first. Eat the *butt*! And make sure to chew it—*slowly!*"

I bit the tail off and started to chew. *Squishy.* I swallowed. "Delicious!" Lucy and Berta looked a bit green.

"Now, Berta, don't be mean, either. You go next. And bite off the head, ears, and snout."

"It's a worm, Sofia, not a pig," said Berta. She closed her eyes, bit, and swallowed. "Gross!"

"Berta, no fair! You didn't chew! It only works if you chew it!"

"Shut up! I can't believe I just ate—Yuck!" I started laughing.

"And, Lucy," said Berta, "you don't have to eat the rest. Forget what Sofia says. She's still making us do crazy things!"

"Lucy, that's right. You don't have to."

"But can I still be a *comadre*?"

"Of course."

"I'll . . . do it too. But I won't chew. Okay?"

"We'll do it when you're older."

"I want to do it now." Lucy took the rest of the tequila worm, shut her eyes tight, and . . . swallowed. "Yuck! Yuck! Yuck!" We all laughed.

Berta reached into her purse and pulled out a Hershey's chocolate bar. "Always prepared!"

Lucy took the first bite.

As I walked through the living room, I noticed a skull with my name on it on the home altar, next to the pictures of dead relatives.

Berta stayed for dinner. Mama's cheese enchiladas were as mouthwatering as I'd remembered. *Way better than the tequila worm!*

During *sobremesa,* Mama mentioned that she had made *pan de muerto* for the Day of the Dead. I looked around and counted—one, two, three, four, five, six crucifixes on the walls.

I wanted to get Terry's voice out of my head—"Don't you think Mexicans are obsessed with death?"

"Sofia," Mama said, "did you hear me?"

I blinked and nodded.

"We all have to be up bright and early tomorrow. Tía Petra has a special surprise for us," she added.

The next morning we were at Tía Petra's by eight. Papa wheeled her into the *sala* on a plastic-covered wheelchair. I gave her a big kiss. Poor Tía Petra had suffered a slight stroke since I'd last seen her. We all sat down and pasted ourselves to her furniture.

"It's time," Tía Petra said. "Before it's too late, I want to give each of you one of my prized possessions. Sofia, I want you to have the armchair. Berta, the sofa . . . See how I've kept it for you!"

She took a pair of scissors and started removing the plastic from the red velvet armchair. As she cut, we saw something start moving on the chair. . . .

Thousands of termites! Swarming everywhere!

Tía Petra shrieked and then started to cry. "I've been a *pendeja*! Call the funeral home! I don't want plastic on my coffin! Just throw me in a hole! Throw the dirt on my face! Let the termites eat me, too!"

We all rushed to hug her.

That evening, Lucy was in the kitchen helping Mama with the turkey *mole* while I visited with the *abuelitos* in the living room. Then the front door opened and Papa wheeled Tía Petra in, her wheelchair no longer in plastic. I kissed her. The front door flew open again. It was Berta. "We're all done with dinner at my house."

"*Ay*, I'm so embarrassed about this morning," said Tía Petra. "And here I was supposed to be tutoring you and Berta, teaching you the mysterious secrets of life. But . . . well, there is a lesson in what you saw today too. More for me than for you, I'm afraid. Yes, not even plastic can prevent . . .

"I should've enjoyed my furniture. I should've let Sofia put *buñuelo* crumbs all over my bare sofa. Let her spill her red hibiscus water all over my table *and* floor . . ." *Boy, I hope this lesson isn't that I'm a messy mule too!* I thought.

She continued. "Yes, by death, we know life. And so

it's best to embrace it. How's that for Martian talk?" Berta and I kissed her. "Now—we eat!"

Our Thanksgiving dinner of turkey *mole*, rice, beans, hot corn tortillas, and *tres leches* cake was to die for.

At *sobremesa*, we were drinking *café de olla*, Papa's sweet spiced coffee treat. Abuelita went first. "Sofia, as the *comadre* in charge of the family's Christmas *nacimiento*, I have the honor of appointing you the Christmas *madrina* this year." Everyone started clapping.

"Eh . . . thank you, Abuelita, but what do I have to do?"

"You'll put baby Jesus in the manger on Christmas and then make him a new dress to wear on the sixth of January."

I looked over at Berta and Lucy.

"Thank you, Abuelita. But can Berta and Lucy help me make the dress?"

"Yes, yes, of course, for this is good training for *comadres*."

I went next at *sobremesa*. "Tía Petra, as I wrote in my letters, Berta and I are getting good at connecting from far away. When are you going to teach us how to connect with the dead?" Berta's eyes widened.

"*Ay*," Tía Petra said, "just wait until you experience being the Christmas *madrina*. This is about learning to kick with your soul, *mi'ja*. Something that the mind—however educated—and even the heart can't do or even begin to understand."

The Christmas Nacimiento

WINTER term classes began the day after Thanksgiving break, and field hockey ended. At last I was playing *soccer* on those emerald fields.

The days before Christmas break rushed by. It was a magical time too, for one morning as I headed up the hill to clean room twenty-four, I found the entire campus, trees, grass, and all, encased in ice, sparkling with the first rays of sun. It was like being inside a glass dome full of snow.

The last day before Christmas break the chapel was aglow with flickering *luminarios* and the altar was surrounded by rows and rows of red poinsettias. It was just like the picture I'd seen in the school brochure. We all sat down to a formal Christmas dinner with china, silver, and crystal, where we ate roast meats and mashed potatoes and ginger cake and were entertained by the school's madrigal group. Then the headmaster stomped in dressed as Santa Claus, saying "Ho! Ho! Ho! "and wishing everyone a merry Christmas and giving out bags of cookies and chocolates.

The next morning Brooke and I exchanged presents: I gave her the novel *One Hundred Years of Solitude*, saying it would give her a taste of the magical; she gave me a book of poems by Emily Dickinson, saying it would give me a taste of the Northeast, home of the Big Three.

Her family dropped me off at the bus station. Marcos and the other valley students were flying home.

I sat in the first row again. How wonderful to be going home, and for Christmas, the most magical time of the year. Then I remembered that I had to be the Christmas *madrina*. Would this teach me to connect with the dead, as Tía Petra had said?

Before dozing off, I smiled, so happy that I'd received honors in all my fall term classes, and that we were now playing soccer. Brooke was hogging the soccer ball; even so, she was nice and fun. I'd been over to her house a couple of times, and her family was warm and friendly.

Marcos and I were good friends now, kicking the

soccer ball almost every Saturday while practicing our Spanish. Sometimes Brooke played too. She laughed when we told her about Johnson's *Ropa Usada* and about my "gorgeous green dress" that she kept borrowing.

I slept most of the trip. Papa, Mama, Lucy, Berta, and Noe were waiting at the station. After we kissed, Mama said, "We have to hurry over to the *abuelitos* to help with the *nacimiento*."

Abuelita was wearing yellow rubber boots and gloves, and standing beside an enormous pile of mud right in the middle of her living room. Her face, glasses, and braided hair were splattered with mud, and the floor was littered with twigs and leaves.

"*Ay*, the Christmas *madrina* has finally arrived!" Abuelita took her gloves off, stomped her boots on the tarp, and gave me a big hug. She started wiping off the mud. "I'm making a Mexican town, *mi'ja*, with a big plaza. It's a replica of the town where my grandmother, who gave you the gift for mule-kicking, met and fell in love with your great-great-grandfather, who gave Berta the gift of those big choppers of hers. First, we will make a four-foot mountain with sprouting tiny trees."

We put pots of cacti, rosemary, and red poinsettias on a plank-and-cinder-block structure, and then filled the spaces with buckets of mud. As we worked, Abuelita told the story of how our great-great-grandparents met:

"My grandfather lived in a tiny town in Mexico, up on a hill, in a two-room house. When I first visited, I was stunned at how small the house was and couldn't believe that six people lived there.

"But what struck me most was how everyone was always so calm and got along. It was because of the town plaza."

Once we finished the mountain, we helped Abuelita create the town, using blocks of Styrofoam and wood painted to look like adobe homes, a church, shops, even a cantina. There were miniature benches, a fountain, and a pink gazebo for the plaza.

Abuelita continued, "The townspeople gathered at the plaza every evening. They sat on the wooden benches, strolled, gossiped, told stories." I remembered Clara, explaining how tales were first told in plazas. "Some sold flowers or fruits from their gardens, or small toys they'd carved, or squares of flan they'd made fresh that day. Others came with guitars and sang songs about love and broken hearts. And this was where recipes and remedies were exchanged, where pictures of babies, *quinceañeras*, and brides, as well as the dead, were passed around.

"And that's where you—Sofia, Berta, Lucy, and Noe—were conjured up too, for that's where my grandfather and grandmother first met and fell in love.

"She was fifteen and had gone to visit her Tía Paula. As was the custom, all the girls in town started walking around the plaza in one direction, while all the boys walked in the opposite direction. He was eighteen, quite handsome, and was carrying a big blue balloon attached to a long stick.

"On the first turn around the plaza, she came face to face with him and his balloon. They smiled at each other. On the next turn, there he was again, now holding only the long stick because his balloon had popped. And on the third turn, he bowed to her and handed her the long stick with a piece of balloon still attached to it."

Once the town was finished, Abuelita reached into her pocket and pulled out a blue balloon. "Here, Lucy, please blow this up, *mi'ja*. It's to honor the love of your great-great-grandparents." Abuelita tied the balloon to a long stick and stuck it inside the plaza.

"Now it's time for a *merienda* of coffee and churros." As we sat at the kitchen table, Mama said, "What this barrio needs is not another fancy TV channel or a new 7-Eleven or even Wal-Mart. No! What it needs is a plaza. Just an open space where the *comadres* can gather in the evenings to talk, look, gossip. And where the young people can meet, just like in Abuelita's story.

"I once heard that if you put too many cats in a house big enough for only one or two cats, the cats eventually go crazy and turn violent. That's exactly what's happening to our barrio.

"Before there was no plaza, but it was nice then, with just our one-family houses all around. The kids played games in each other's yards, kickball in the alley, soccer in the street."

Abuelita said, "It was one big family, with everyone knowing each other and everyone pitching in and looking after each other's kids. The old ones were always telling tales and stories. And when they died, the family would lay them out on a table in the *sala* and retell their tales, until it was finally time to plant them in the ground. Now apartments are taking over."

I said, "Oh, but it still feels so good to be home."

On December 21, we all gathered at the *abuelitos'* house. Abuelita had added a wooden *jacal* to the plaza. It was made from pieces of mesquite and had a ceramic Mary and Joseph—each about a foot high and badly chipped and faded—kneeling before an empty cradle.

Ten cardboard boxes marked EL NACIMIENTO stood where the tarp and mound of mud had been.

After a cup of frothy Mexican chocolate and a handful of *pan de polvo* cookies—each star, bell, and angel sprinkled with crystals of sugar and freshly ground cinnamon— Abuelita carefully opened the first box. It was filled with balls of old newspaper.

I wondered what pieces I would find. Year after year, each of us selected a ball, unwrapped it to discover the piece inside, and went to Abuelita, who stood in front of the *nacimiento* like a conductor before a symphony. She would take the piece, examine it through her thick eyeglasses, and then tell us where to put it.

Each piece had its own story about who had given it to her and when. A piece might make the *nacimiento* one year but not the next. It depended on how Abuelita was inspired to decorate the *nacimiento* that year.

The only pieces she put out herself were those of Mary and Joseph. They were the oldest.

Abuelita took Mary in her hands. She traced her face, her veil, her entire outline with her long fingers. "This piece makes me feel as if my mother and grandmother are right in the room with me. It makes me feel like a little girl again, when I was helping them create the Christmas *nacimiento*. I've since discovered that creating the *nacimiento* isn't work, really, even when it takes weeks, for it's a gift of sacredness— to the baby, to the whole family."

I unwrapped one ball and laughed. The gray ceramic elephant with the pink saddle! I'd chosen it in other years. "Now, that," Abuelita said, "belongs to one of the three magi. Put it at the very bottom of the hill, for the three magi aren't coming for a while."

The next piece I unwrapped was a lime green plastic dinosaur with a long goofy neck. This used to be my favorite, but now it seemed only gaudy and silly: did it really belong in the *nacimiento*? But it was also one of Abuelita's favorites, a gift from Mama when she was a little girl. Abuelita said, "Put it right next to Mary, just outside the *jacal*, with its long neck peeking in."

And that's how it went for hours, box after box. There must have been more than seventy angels—some flying, others kneeling or sleeping; and many with chipped wings and cracked faces; and three with no heads at all. There were hundreds of animals: pigs and ponies, storks and camels, even a pink flamingo and a big ceramic whale that went in a pool of wadded-up blue plastic.

There were the usual shepherds, about thirty of them, and the three magi—one a foot high; the second, five inches; and the third, only the size of a thimble. There were twelve plastic mariachis, each equipped with a tiny violin, horn, or guitar; a huge ceramic Cantinflas, with his pants falling down, chomping on an onion, as well as a bobbing head of JFK and a hula-dancing Hawaiian girl in a bright grass skirt. There were cut-out pictures of Maria Felix, Pancho Villa, Emiliano Zapata, and the Virgin of Guadalupe.

And then there were the inexplicable: two big stuffed green frogs, one playing an accordion, the other, a trumpet; as well as bottle caps, glass marbles, maracas, Mexican jumping beans, tiny piñatas, plastic whistles, cardboard dolls in acrobat outfits, a dried-up pomegranate, an enormous lollipop with a tequila worm inside, and another tequila worm in a tiny bottle of mescal. There were rocks and shells and paper flowers and bows and all kinds of Mama's wacky handmade things too.

Abuelita added a big yellow pineapple, five red apples, three oranges, half a dozen green chilies, and a handful of cinnamon sticks and walnuts.

Then we put wisps of angel hair here, there, and everywhere.

Abuelita disappeared behind the mountain, and hundreds of tiny lights, red, yellow, green, and blue, winked on to sparkle throughout the mountain, town, and plaza. Every piece came to life.

Over another cup of hot chocolate, but this time with a crispy cinnamon-covered *buñuelo* each, we all sat around the *nacimiento* and Abuelita told stories of how her grandmother and then her mother had created the *nacimiento* each year. Sometimes it was Bethlehem, or a Mexican village, once, a lush African jungle, with wild animals and exotic plants. Often it took weeks to finish. I shook my head. How tired I was from just putting the pieces out!

Before we left that night, Abuelita took me aside and handed me a small bag made of white satin. "Here, *mi'ja*, love him like he's your own baby."

When I unwrapped it at home, I found a mended, glued, and badly chipped ceramic baby Jesus. Mama said, "Your great-grandmother gave him to your grandmother when she was appointed the Christmas *madrina* the very first time."

The next morning I called Berta. "*Comadre*, I need your help. The doll is falling apart. Do you think we can find a tiny dress at Johnson's *Ropa Usada . . .*"

Mama walked in. "Sofia, hang up. I need to talk to you—*now!*"

Berta said, "Oh, Sofia, you're in *trouble.*"

"Yes, Mama."

"Sit down." *Oh, no!*

"I heard you talking to Berta. This is no joke, being the Christmas *madrina.* If you can't take this seriously, tell your *abuelita* right now. You are representing the whole family, Sofia."

"But Mama, I wasn't—"

"Remember how your papa makes his beans sacred by how he cleans and cooks them?"

"Yes."

"Well, start there."

"What do you mean?"

"Make this so-called doll your baby by cleaning and gluing him back together, carefully and thoughtfully. This is not the panty-hose baby, Sofia."

"But what about the diaper, the dress?"

"Here." Mama pulled a square of white satin and another of purple from a bag. "Use this." She left as Lucy and Berta walked in.

"Are you in the doghouse?" asked Lucy.

"Sort of."

Berta said, "Oh, you should've heard her on the phone, Lucy, saying she wanted to buy a tiny dress for Jesus at Johnson's and—"

"Well, I wasn't joking, but I now get how this

experience is going to teach me to connect with the dead: I'm going to *join* them!"

Berta and Lucy started laughing.

"*Shhhh!* Mama is going to flip again."

"So how can we help?" said Lucy.

"Well, get me some glue and a towel. I'll get a big bowl and soap. Let's bathe him and then glue him up!"

And after baby Jesus was all clean and freshly glued and sweet smelling, we took him over to Berta's house and started making his new diaper and dress.

Berta and Lucy measured, traced, cut, and sewed while I counted buttons, picked up pins, and fetched whatever they wanted. I also talked to the baby, telling him funny stories about Berta and Lucy. That night he slept on my pillow.

I became so attached to him that I wanted to take him back to school with me. How strange to feel such enormous affection for a *doll*!

After *Misa de Gallo* on Christmas Eve, we gathered for a prayer in front of the *nacimiento,* and I placed baby Jesus in the mesquite cradle. He was wearing his new white satin diaper.

We sat around the glowing *nacimiento,* our plates piled high with Mama's pork-filled Christmas tamales. We ate bowls and bowls of hot, hearty *menudo.*

On the sixth of January, we gathered again at the *nacimiento*. After Abuelita placed the three magi at the manger, along with their steeds—the chunky elephant, a red camel, and a pink plastic horse—we said another prayer, and then I took baby Jesus and carefully dressed him in the new purple satin dress. I walked around the room and presented him to everyone to kiss.

Later we feasted on *pozole* and took turns cutting a slice from the *pan de rosca*, shaped like a king's crown and sparkling with jewels of candied fruit.

That night I found it hard to leave baby Jesus behind. I also felt strangely comforted by this ritual, which seemed mad at first—what with the mountain of mud and the thousand strange pieces. It was somewhat like Clara and her bag of things and stories, except the *nacimiento* seemed to conjure up not only long-gone relatives, but also the sacred, the holy, something I never experienced at Saint Luke's.

"*Mi'ja*," Papa said before bed, "that little *nacimiento* conjured up baby Jesus. I *feel* his peaceful presence every-where. So when I'm gone, remember to conjure me up by sitting down and cleaning a pound of pinto beans for me, just like we always do."

I laughed and then kissed him goodnight.

TEQUILA WORM

AFTER that first term, it got easier going back and forth between school and home.

I especially *loved* going home for the summer. I worked teaching summer school but spent plenty of my time escaping the heat driving around with Berta and Lucy. By the summer after junior year, we had eaten *seven* tequila worms!

Lucy was growing up so fast and was now helping Berta plan her wedding. I still thought Berta ought to be thinking about college, not marriage, but I'd never seen her so happy. Mama was still making wacky things. But Papa seemed tired. He was getting paler and paler.

That summer before my senior year I turned off the bedroom light one night and was about to tell Lucy a funny story when she said into the dark, "Sofia, Papa's not well."

"What do you mean?"

"He's been going through tests."

"What's wrong with him?"

"They don't know. Sofia, you can't say anything about this. He doesn't want you to worry. He even made me promise not to tell you. But you should *know*. It's nothing, he says, just part of turning into a *viejito*. So promise, Sofia?"

"Okay."

I couldn't sleep that night.

The next day was Tuesday, but when Papa came home from work, he went to sit out on the porch.

"Papa," I said. "Aren't we going to clean beans? It's *Tuesday*." He did look gray.

"Ah, yes, *mi'ja*. Let's clean our beans." He got up slowly.

"Papa, are you feeling all right?"

"Yes, yes. Your papa is just getting a little older. That's all." He forced a smile.

"Papa, sit down. I'll get the beans." Papa lowered himself into a chair at the kitchen table. I opened the metal container, expecting Papa to dip his hand in, but he kept staring at the table.

"Papa, are you sick? *Please* tell me."

"No, no, *mi'ja*. Just a little tired." He smiled weakly and dipped his hand in. "*Mi'ja,* it's *so* good to have you home. I'm *so* proud of you. You're doing well at that school."

"Papa . . . should I come home? Do you want me to come back home?"

"Back home?"

"Yes, I'm sure I can transfer to McHi for my senior year. . . ."

"But why, *mi'ja?* I thought you liked that school. And what about applying to Harvard?"

"Yes, Papa, but . . . you don't seem well. I don't care about school."

Papa made himself laugh. "I'm fine, just fine. JFK went to Harvard—right?"

"Yes."

"*Mi'ja,* that would be a wonderful dream: my daughter going to the same college as JFK."

I left for senior year, only after assurances from Mama that Papa would get checked through and through.

I worked harder than ever, always thinking about Papa. I was second in my class, cocaptain of the soccer team, dorm proctor, even class president.

I kept calling home. In early October, the doctors decided to send Papa to the VA hospital in San Antonio to see some specialists.

That Saturday I took the bus to San Antonio, then a

taxi to the VA hospital. Mama, Lucy, and Berta were in a room with Papa.

"*Ay, mi'ja,* it's good to see you," said Papa, sitting up in bed, in blue pajamas. I kissed him. He'd lost so much weight, and all his color. "I can't wait to get back home, the food here is *terrible*."

I didn't want to go back to school that Sunday, but Papa said, "Don't worry, *mi'ja*. I'll be fine. I'm just here for tests. Go study hard for your papa. I've already told everybody you're going to Harvard, just like JFK."

The following Friday, Mr. Smith came to get me in English class. "Sofia, I'm so sorry. Your father is not doing well."

Papa's brown and white boots: those were the first things I saw upon entering the hospital room. They stood beside the metal bed.

Papa's dark, piercing Zapata eyes were closed. He lay there in a thin gown, sleeping, with Mama and Lucy beside him.

I started to cry.

I took his right hand, opened his long, warm fingers, and noticed that the lines on his palm were the exact ones etched in mine. His teeth were still perfect, so white and even. How could a cancer be destroying something so beautiful, this wonderful man? Just weeks before he'd

been out dancing with Mama. Now he was terminal—
days left, perhaps only hours.

There were pictures Scotch-taped to the wall above
him: one of him and me cleaning beans at the kitchen
table, another of him dancing with Mama, and a third of
him carrying Lucy as a baby.

His right arm was purple and bloated like a melon
from an IV feeding him. Another IV dripped morphine.

Suddenly his breathing stopped and then started up
again with a loud gasp. I ran for the doctor, who put an
oxygen mask on Papa. "His lungs are full of liquid," he
said. He rolled in a machine and connected a clamp to
Papa's thumb. The machine clocked at 130 heartbeats per
minute. "He's fighting for his life."

I continued to hold Papa's hand while Mama held the
other. Lucy stood at his side, looking lost. A nurse came
in. "Talk to him," she said. "Yes, go ahead and talk to him.
He can still hear you. Hearing is the last thing to go, even
in a coma."

When the nurse left, Mama leaned over and started
whispering into Papa's ear. She told him how much we all
loved him. She started humming "Julia." Lucy began to cry.

I turned and saw Tía Belia, Berta's mother, sitting in
the corner, praying her rosary.

She got up and walked over to me. She made the sign
of the cross and whispered, "*Mi'ja,* I need to talk to you."
Lucy took Papa's hand. I hugged Lucy and then followed
Tía Belia out the door.

In the hallway, Tía Belia said, "*Mi'ja*, it's time to let your papa go. He's staying for you, out of concern. Let him go rest now."

Stunned, I didn't know what to say. How did she know? I recalled that Papa had said that Tía Belia, the *curandera*, had cured Lucy of *susto*, something the rich doctors hadn't been able to do.

When I returned to the room, I gently stroked Papa's hair and then leaned close to him. My tears rained on his eyes. I told him that I loved him very, very deeply. Then, after a long, long pause, I said it was time for him to go rest, that he had been a good and wonderful papa, and that I promised to now take care of Mama and Lucy. I glanced up. Mama looked stunned. Lucy was crying harder.

The numbers on the machine started falling faster and faster. I ran for the doctor. At forty heartbeats per minute, the priest came in and gave Papa his last rites.

The machine stopped at zero. Tía Belia, with Berta, returned out of the blue. We held hands around Papa's body and prayed and cried for a long, long time.

When we left his side late that night, I reached down, took Papa's beautiful brown and white boots, and hugged them. I wanted to die. But Mama smiled and then wove her warm arms around Lucy and me and held us for a long time, like a tree giving life to her fruit.

When we finally got home to McAllen, I walked straight into the kitchen and took out Papa's beans. I sat down at the table, opened the container, and started cleaning. Mama, Lucy, and Berta sat down and started cleaning beans too. As I worked, I *did* feel Papa's presence. We cooked them and we each ate a cup of whole beans in his honor.

The next day we went to bury him at the cemetery. And there on his fresh grave, I left Papa a cup of whole beans, along with a tiny spoon, just the way he liked them.

The day after Papa's funeral I walked into the living room and was choked by the overwhelming smell of flowers everywhere—on the dining room table, on the coffee table, on the chairs, on the floor.

I found Mama moving vases all around. "Please help me. We need to make room for the rosary tonight. Remember, it takes a total of nine days for a soul to get to heaven." I nodded. The first rosary had been at the funeral home. Tonight would be the second.

That evening, Mama's closest *comadres,* all twelve of them, including Abuelita, Tía Belia, Tía Petra, and Clara, as well as Lucy and Berta, gathered around the coffee table.

Mama lit a votive candle and placed it in the middle of the table. This was to light Papa's way into heaven. It would stay lit for the next seven days. She placed a full glass of water beside the candle, for Papa to drink on his journey. Next to it she placed the silver crucifix that had hung on the lid of Papa's open casket, as well as the folded-up American flag that had been presented to her at the burial.

Mama opened a small paper bag and gave a rosary to those who hadn't brought one. She made the sign of the cross and began. We took turns leading a set of prayers, each consisting of one Our Father and ten Hail Marys. Once the rosary was over, we all embraced. Then the *comadres* told stories about Papa and about their papas, while drinking Mexican chocolate and eating pumpkin empanadas. I was still so numb that I barely managed to stay awake.

And that was how it was for the next seven days.

The morning after the ninth rosary, Mama, Lucy, Berta, and I sat and cleaned another pound of beans at the kitchen table. As we did, I felt Papa nearby. I ate my cup of whole beans, enjoying them as he had. Then I was able to board the bus back to Austin.

When I started up the stairs to my dorm, I had to stop and sit on the steps. It was difficult to breathe. Somehow the presence of my family and the *comadres* had shielded me from the enormous sense of loss and aloneness I was now feeling. I was feeling my mortality for the first time. It was like being completely lost in a sea of overwhelming darkness.

The time had finally come to open the secret *cascarone*

that Papa had given me on my fifteenth birthday. I got up and went to my room. I fetched Papa's secret *cascarone* from my room altar, put it inside my shirt pocket, and went and sat down on one of the steps outside.

I took it out and traced the drawing of the world, the stars that Papa had colored more than two years before. Then I carefully peeled off the paper crown on top and broke off a few pieces of eggshell around the small hole.

I slowly tipped the egg over, and out spilled three wooden objects. They were very similar to the Saint Sofia he had carved for me. I looked inside the egg and saw a piece of paper. I took it out and unfolded it.

Mi'ja, *here's a little secret about Saint Sofia, your patron saint, who represents, as you know, divine wisdom. She had three wonderful daughters, who were martyred for their passion just as she was. They were Faith, Love, and Charity. Create joy and magic in life by weaving these three into your life experiences too. Your papa, who will always be with you.*

I started to cry. But I turned and saw the green playing fields in the distance, and the blue sky above, and then Brooke came down the stairs and hugged me.

That spring I saw how Papa's death had shifted my focus entirely, my whole life. Yes, I still wanted to get into a good college, but life was more than that now. I was writing stories to conjure up Papa, and these stories, especially, had opened up a whole new world for me.

THᴇ TᴇQᴜɪLᴀ WORM

But college was all my friends could think of. Brooke had only applied to Brown, saying she was sick of hearing about Harvard, Yale, and Princeton. Marcos had applied to the University of Texas, wanting to stay near home.

When the letters finally came, I stood at my mailbox and found that I had indeed gotten into the big three, but I knew with my soul I would gladly trade getting accepted for just being with Papa. Brooke and Marcos ran up to me, waving their acceptance letters.

One Saturday I was in my room writing a story about Papa and me waltzing to "Julia" when Brooke and Marcos peered through the window.

"Time for soccer," said Marcos.

"Eh . . . thanks, but . . ." Brooke leaned in and pulled me by the arm. She dragged me outside through the window, where Marcos grabbed my other arm. Then Brooke went back inside and returned with a paper bag. They marched me to the soccer field.

We kicked the ball around, running up and down like crazy people, yelling, Brooke hogging the ball as usual. But now I knew tricks to get it away from her. It felt good to move, to get air, to see the green fields again.

Breathless, we fell onto the grass, looking up at the sky.

"Sofia." Brooke sat up, pulling a book out of the paper bag. It was the book of poems by Emily Dickinson she'd given me for Christmas. "This poem really helped me when I lost my grandmother. I'm hoping it'll help you, too. Listen:

"A wounded deer leaps highest,
I've heard the hunter tell;
'Tis but the ecstasy of death,
And then the brake is still.

"The smitten rock that gushes,
The trampled steel that springs:
A cheek is always redder
Just where the hectic stings!

"Mirth is the mail of anguish,
In which it caution arm,
Lest anybody spy the blood
And 'You're hurt' exclaim!

Somehow the pain of losing my grandmother has made me appreciate living more."

"My turn now," Marcos said. He unwrapped a disk of Ibarra chocolate and held it to my lips. "Take a big bite, Sofia. It really works! Trust me! It'll make you feel like you're right there in McAllen, dancing with your papa."

I laughed and took a bite. "It's a wonder you still have any teeth left. This stuff is *hard*."

Then Brooke pulled out the tiny bottle with the tequila worm inside, the one Papa had sent me years ago.

"Okay, Sofia, it's time. You're starting to go around like a ghost. It's time to take your papa's ultimate cure for homesickness." Marcos popped the tequila worm out of the bottle and dangled it.

"Only if you two take a bite too." They looked queasy. "I'm serious. And I'll take the middle, since I've had the head and butt before. I want to finally eat the whole tequila worm."

So Marcos bit the head off, Brooke the butt, and then I popped the soul of the tequila worm in my mouth and started chewing slowly.

"*Ay!* Sofia!" Marcos said, "This works better than eating three disks of chocolate. I don't feel homesick for McAllen or anyone anymore." He looked at me with his bright dark eyes and then kissed my check. We all laughed and hugged each other.

As we walked back to the dorm, I did feel lighter, relieved, so glad to have such friends.

I thought of Papa's bean cleaning and cooking, about the Christmas *nacimiento,* and about the nine days of rosaries to get Papa's soul to heaven. These were all rituals that connected me to something higher. And now, eating the tequila worm had worked its own power.

As I climbed the steps to my room, I smiled, feeling—with my soul—that *now* I could finally begin the tequila worm story for Papa.

The Plaza

YEARS later I returned to my old barrio for a visit.

I was living in San Francisco, where I worked as a civil rights attorney, writing stories every chance I got. Lucy was a schoolteacher in Austin. Berta still lived in McAllen, with Jamie and their two boys. We called and visited each other all the time.

Mama was right, though: our barrio was nothing like I remembered it.

As the kids I had played with had grown up and moved away and most of their grandparents and then parents had taken ill and died, the simple clapboard houses had been torn down and replaced by one- and two-story apartment buildings. Our barrio had faded away, and gangs and graffiti had moved in.

The few original families still living there, mostly quite old, didn't feel safe anymore, but what could they do? It was as if the city were deliberately destroying the barrio by putting far too many people there. The old families didn't have anything against the new people: most were hardworking and were only trying to survive. But to pile six families on a lot that had once housed one was *loco*.

Years back I had moved Mama to a safer house in town.

We drove to the old house, and Mama and I started picking up the broken glass in the yard. "Mama, what do you want done with the house?"

She shrugged. "*Ay, mi'ja,* I hate the thought of selling it to only have another apartment built. It's such a rough place now." She shook her head and sighed.

"I loved visiting all my *comadres* and sharing plates of food and picking fresh limes from Doña Virginia's tree. We were always sharing, trading, borrowing chilies, cribs, tamales. There was such a calmness then too, and it was especially nice in the evenings when it cooled and the scent of orange blossoms sweetened the air.

"Remember," she continued, "how this was the time

when all the families came out to their porches, especially when Clara was in town with her big bag of stories? And it was especially nice when the full moon shone and the sky dazzled with stars.

"Now the new buildings block the sky. Trucks screech and radios blare.

"And to think I once dreamed that you and Lucy and Berta would grow up and settle here too, so we could always continue being one big family."

I nodded, hugging Mama.

And that is how it all began. We drove city hall and the mayor crazy, telling them that they were destroying our families, our barrios, and our future by letting more and more apartments be built, that it was like putting too many cats in one house. We called and wrote letters to all the families and neighbors who'd since moved out.

Then I bought one house, tore it down, and built a new brick house for Mama. As for our old house, I had it torn down too, but there I created a little space, with orange trees on each corner and plantings of roses, hibiscus, beautiful red and purple bougainvillea, and in Papa's memory, Mexican jasmine. There were wooden benches, too, and even a small wooden gazebo at the very center that I painted bright pink. I built a tall white picket fence all around it and bolted the gate shut.

I made keys to the *placita* and gave a key to each of the

old families still living there. When I visited, I saw that slowly, slowly, they started coming to sit there, to talk, to see each other. They started to help water the plants and trees and cut the grass. I'd find seven, sometimes ten people sitting and talking in the evenings. They said it reminded them of long ago, and that the scent of the orange blossoms, Mexican jasmine, and roses brought back sweet memories of their childhoods and the plazas in the towns where they'd grown up.

Then little by little they started inviting some of the new families to the *placita* too. One Sunday afternoon, I saw some of these new young faces strumming guitars and singing love songs in the pink gazebo. I saw families, fresh from Mass, enjoying picnics of tacos and roasted chicken, sitting on blankets on the new-mown grass. That day I blew up a blue balloon and attached it to the gazebo.

Only a year later I received a call from Mama. "*Mi'ja,* would you please take the fence down? Everyone knows each other now—so it's just in the way."

After that call, I flew to McAllen and we pulled the fence down. Then I took the four little wooden saints from my pocket, the ones Papa had carved for me years before. I prayed that the rituals I'd experienced as a child—the very ones that Mama, Papa, and the *comadres* had worked so hard to instill in me—would be nourished and shared and spread from the heart of that little plaza.

It had taken years, many years, for me to finally see the true meaning of becoming a good *comadre*. The first glimmer of this was after Papa died so suddenly. His death had completely flipped my world upside down. But Mama had kept her balance and serenity in this darkest of times, because of her *comadres*.

Later that year, I went home for the Day of the Dead. Mama, Lucy, Berta, Jamie, Noe, Tía Belia, Berta's father, and I prayed and then placed a dozen hot tamales and a cup of freshly made pinto beans on Papa's grave. I smiled, for now I understood that it was not an obsession with death that Mexicans had after all, but rather an acceptance of it—woven like a thick vine throughout our lives, helping us transcend death itself and compelling us to live even richer, more meaningful lives.

That evening we all gathered again on the porch of Mama's new house, and I brought out Clara's old burlap bag. I reached inside to pull out a small paper box and took out Papa's secret *cascarone,* the one I had finally opened at Saint Luke's. It was not filled with confetti, but rather with all the memories of Papa and of our lives together as a family, a barrio, and as *comadres* and *compadres*.

And as Papa's secret *cascarone* went from hand to hand, person to person, we vowed that we would always come together to create the family's Christmas *nacimiento* each year. Now the responsibility had passed on to Mama.

Before I went to bed, I called my *comadre* Brooke and my *compadre* Marcos and told them the happy news, that Mama had just appointed me the Christmas *madrina* for the year.

Viola Canales, a native of McAllen, Texas, is a graduate of Harvard College and Harvard Law School. She was a captain in the U.S. Army and has worked as a community organizer for the United Farm Workers; as a trial lawyer; as a regional administrator for the U.S. Small Business Administration in the Southwestern United States, Guam, and Hawaii; and as a senior executive of a corporation focusing on enhancing the success of women and minority CEOs. She lives in Stanford, California.

Viola Canales is the author of *Orange Candy Slices and Other Secret Tales,* a collection of stories. *The Tequila Worm* is her first novel.